SHADOW STALKER

THE GHOST REAPERS SERIES
BOOK 2

IAN FORTEY
AND
RON RIPLEY

EDITED BY ANNE LAO
AND DAWN KLEMISH

ISBN: 979-8-89476-276-0
Copyright © 2024 by ScareStreet.com

All rights reserved. This book or any portion thereof may not be reproduced or used in any manner whatsoever without written permission from the publisher except for the use of brief quotations in a book review.

This is a work of fiction. Any resemblance to actual persons, living or dead, or actual events is purely coincidental.

Enter the Realm of Terror...

We'd like to take a moment to thank you for your support and invite you to join our VIP newsletter.

Dive deeper into the darkness with exclusive offers, early access to new releases, and bone-chilling deals when you sign up at www.ScareStreet.com.

Let the nightmares begin…

See you in the shadows,
Scare Street

Prologue

High in the trees, the bass thrum of a Eurasian eagle owl's call broke through the stillness. The black forest lay hidden beneath the canopy even from the light of the moon. Only the smallest of cracks allowed hints of the sky to break through.

A twig snapped. The massive owl left its perch and meter-wide wings silently carried it beyond sight to darker, deeper parts of the woods.

The nights in the north had grown cold. The southern cities were still hot in the day, under the blazing sun, but the forests of the north, only broken up haphazardly by small villages and towns, were subject to those Siberian cold fronts that swept down unpredictably throughout the year.

It was more than eight hours by car in any given direction to find a town with more than a thousand people in it. But that did not mean there were no signs of life. Or death.

Spirits wandered the forest. In the year 1225 AD, two great armies made the forest and surrounding countryside the site of a great battle. The invading force from the east had thought to flank its enemy by traveling north through the woods and attacking from the rear. But a spy had sent word ahead of time, and their enemy met them in the forest where their horse-mounted bowmen were rendered all but useless and their superior numbers were spread thin and disorganized.

History said ten thousand men died in that forest alone. The restless dead still wandered the night, bound to their helms, their swords, their signets, and their bones. But they are a quiet dead, and they long ago stopped caring about the plight of life and the living.

Three of the figures that wandered the darkened woods were not dead though. Drawn to Northern Vakovia in pursuit of prey, each man looked like a walking shadow. Dressed head to toe in black, armed with assault rifles and the most advanced tactical gear, these were not simple hunters. These were Reapers.

It was impossible to navigate the woods soundlessly. Even the most adept of the Reapers, trained in tracking and espionage techniques, could not avoid the shuffle of dead leaves, the snapping of the smallest twigs, and the rustling of movement in a forest more still than a grave.

Few living things made the forest home. The dead kept life at bay. In the many years since the great battle had claimed so many, only a few creatures had adapted to the unnatural still. Birds in the trees. Insects in the earth. Silent things that evaded even death's eyes.

The dense trees cut the wind, preventing even the ambient sound of rustling leaves. "As still as the grave" was an expression people used, and it was true. The nameless forest betrayed even the quietest of indiscretions.

Spread out around the three men, three more figures moved through the woods. Unlike the soldiers, these three made no sound. Their feet passed through piles of leaves and fallen branches untouched.

Reapers called them spectral assets. Ghosts who served alongside the living. They hunted and killed in exchange for freedom. A bound spirit could never travel more than a mile from the object that held it rooted to the living world. But those recruited by Reaper Company traveled where their living partners traveled. They could see the world and be a part of it like no other spirit could. For those who didn't care about taking lives, joining up was a simple choice to make.

"There's nothing here," the lead ghost hissed.

He was stocky and intimidating, with eyes the color of fresh blood. His lower lip had been torn off down to the chin, exposing his jaw and bloody gums in a way that made him look like savage. He walked hunched over, almost lumbering, and had arms the size of a normal man's legs.

"Keep it down, Zef," his human companion admonished.

The big ghost stopped and turned to look back. The three soldiers were hidden behind night vision goggles, but he always knew where his partner, Lerner, was. He could feel the pull of his haunted item, stashed in a pocket on the man's side.

"It's been weeks," the ghost growled. "If he's not dead, he's left the country."

"You have your orders," Lerner said.

Zef had only become Lerner's partner the month before. Before Reaper Company came calling, he was a resident of Big Mac, the Oklahoma State Penitentiary. He'd been scheduled to die by the electric chair in 1964 but ended up getting killed on the yard. He took the other guy with him.

Over half a century he'd been on the prison grounds, until a suit covered in military medals showed up and plucked his haunted item, a Bozo the Clown Pez dispenser, from a box of junk left in storage. The man made him an offer, and he accepted. But he never expected to be wasting his freedom wandering forests on the other side of the world for weeks on end. Better to have stayed in the Oklahoma prison; at least there were fights to watch.

The ghosts of the forest offered no answers. None of them spoke English, and even what could be translated was useless. They were too old, some more than a century, and they all seemed trapped in their memories.

The three living men split up, each taking a new quadrant to search. Their coverage of the forest was systematic. Zef thought it was dumb. The woods had to be hundreds of acres. Three men and three ghosts couldn't search it all, and even if they did, their coverage area was too small. Their target could slip past them a hundred times over.

Zef watched the other spirits drift away with their partners. They were as dull as the living they worked with. Soldiers seemed stupid to him, just fools who allowed someone else to boss them around. Taking orders had never been Zef's strong suit. He preferred doing whatever he wanted whenever he wanted. That was how he ended up in prison.

They delved deeper into the woods. Lerner had night vision and thermal scanners to find anything alive among the trees. The monotony of it all was lost on him. The man was alive, he only had a finite time to be alive, and he still wasn't bored. Zef didn't like him at all. He played nice while he had to. He followed rules. Said things like "Yes, sir." He resisted the urge to rip people's throats out.

When they got to a place where he wanted to be, a proper city somewhere like Paris or London or New York, things would change. He'd take Lerner out somewhere secret, just the two of them. He'd make up a story. He found a target, or a pile of money, or whatever it took.

He'd get Lerner alone, and he'd gut him. He'd pull his insides out like he was gutting a pig and watch the man's life wash across the floor in a stinking wave of guts and blood. And wherever he fell, wherever his body crumpled and rotted, that would be where that Bozo the Clown Pez dispenser would spend forever. That would be Zef's new home for all time. He'd have to choose wisely.

Zef could not feel the cold, but he'd heard the Reapers complaining about it. They'd just come from Ravjek, which was sweltering hot, and now it felt like fall. They called themselves soldiers. They acted like badasses when a group of them was together. Now, they complained about the weather. Zef had no idea how the group had come together.

The many ghosts in the forest were a constant distraction. The moment Zef saw movement, he thought their endless hunt was over, but it turned out to be an ancient warrior stabbed through the heart, searching for his lost comrades.

"This will take years if it ever works at all," Zef said.

They needed more men if they planned to succeed. It was simple math, and he didn't understand why they were wasting their time. There were not enough Reapers to scour the entire country of Vakovia. They should have just let it go.

There was no reply from Lerner, not even one of his dour "do your job" retorts that bored Zef so. He turned to look back at the soldier only to find him gone.

"Lerner?"

Zef stood next to a twisted, half-bent hornbeam tree and scanned the darkness. He did not need light to see the way the living did, but there was no sign of the man who had been just a few paces behind him a moment earlier.

"Lerner!"

He lumbered back the way he had come and circled around an English walnut with boughs that hung nearly to the ground. Lerner's body lay slumped beneath it, his head twisted halfway around.

Zef stared into the man's open eyes. They were still wide but unfocused, simply gazing up at the black sky above.

"Katz! Lorenzo!" Zef bellowed.

Neither of the two soldiers answered his call.

"Venti! Shalomar!"

The other spectral assets did not reply either. Zef growled and flexed his big hands.

"You're going to regret this," the ghost muttered, stalking around the tree, and peering through the low-hanging boughs and tangle of branches. He did not need backup from the living or other ghosts. He never needed help to kill. He never would.

Whoever had killed Lerner had done so in seconds and vanished without a sound. There were spirits around, but they were all clad in clothing from a bygone era and were as lost as any spirit Zef had seen. They were not killers anymore.

Someone else was in the woods. Their target, it seemed, had found them instead of the other way around. Zef was now the hunted.

He circled the tree, and something to his right caught his eye. Maybe thirty yards away, a shape ducked low near some underbrush. He approached without making a sound, creeping from tree trunk to tree trunk, in the places where living eyes could not see.

It was a man crouched low to the ground, hidden in bushes near the base of an oak, dressed in the same tactical gear as the Reapers. The helmet on his head was not obscured enough, not hidden from Zef's dead eyes.

The ghost made no sound as he slipped his arm around his prey's throat. Only there was no throat. The helmet was propped up on a stick, same as the tactical vest.

The helmet fell, rustling the leaves. It came to rest next to Lorenzo's body. His neck was broken the same as Lerner's, a thin trickle of blood running from his mouth into the leaves of the forest floor.

Zef growled and turned away from the bushes, ready to venture west in search of Katz. A figure in the dark stood behind him.

"The woods are dangerous at night," the man said. He was bald, devoid of even eyebrows, and his face was a patchwork of scars. Zef recognized him from the photos the Reapers were issued. Their target. Shane Ryan.

The man's fist shot out and took Zef square in the nose. Zef reeled back, stunned beyond words as the blow caused his head to vibrate. It was not pain he felt—he was long beyond that—but it was a real, physical blow to his face. It had pressure behind it. Power. It made his nose crunch audibly and bend to one side.

In his skull, Zef felt the cartilage shift and crumble. He was aware that his nose had shifted position and shape.

"You broke my nose," he gasped.

Ryan punched him again, this time in the jaw, right in the exposed teeth where his lip had once been.

Another crunch and three of his teeth buckled and fell into his mouth. They felt like pebbles on his tongue, and he spit them out, watching as they faded from existence before they even hit the ground. They did not reappear in his mouth. The damage Ryan inflicted on the dead were permanent. The things he'd heard about him were true. He could hurt the dead.

"It's not possible," Zef muttered, backing off before the man could take another strike.

Zef had traveled from Oklahoma to the other side of the planet and that godforsaken forest because he was promised freedom. He had a plan to get out. He was going to get to a place he always wanted to be, to a big city full of life and excitement. That was his plan. That was going to be his eternity.

"Katz! Shalomar!" he roared, running from the bald man through the woods.

He could hear Ryan behind him, his feet crunching leaves and breaking sticks. He was fast and persistent.

"Venti!" he shouted, trying to find the other ghosts.

"You have no friends left," Ryan yelled after him. He laughed then and Zef gritted the teeth he had left. He was laughing. There was no way he'd killed three Reapers and two ghosts that quickly. There was no way. He was just one man.

"Shalomar!" he roared again.

A ghost appeared ahead of him, moving between the trees. Zef angled toward it.

"He's coming! He's alone, but he killed Lerner and Lorenzo. Help me!"

The spirit in the trees stepped out where Zef could see him. It was neither Shalomar nor Venti, and it definitely wasn't one of the lost spirits of the woods.

"Who said he's alone?" the ghost asked.

The spirit was a short, thin man with a deep scar from one side of his throat to the other and smudges of dirt across his face.

"Who the hell are you?"

"He is Radek," someone else said. The voice came from behind him, and Zef turned to face a spirit even larger than himself. He was shirtless and covered in thick hair across his broad chest and arms. An unruly beard hung halfway down his chest, and one of his ears was missing, as was an eye.

"I am Oleg," the monster said, patting his chest. He smiled at Zef, and the expression held no kindness.

"What the hell is this?" Zef asked.

"This is the end of the line," Ryan said, joining them from behind the one called Oleg.

"No," Zef said. "No, this isn't fair. I had a plan."

"So did I," Ryan countered.

"They're gonna kill you, Ryan. They're gonna gut you in the goddamn forest, and you're going to deserve it."

The bald man shrugged.

A sound broke through the darkness then. A high-pitched whine zipped through the shadows. Ryan cursed and turned sharply, grabbing his face. Blood flowed from a scrape across his cheek where a bullet had grazed him.

Zef laughed. The second team had arrived.

"You're going to die!" the ghost spat.

"You first," Ryan said. He took Zef's head in his hands as Oleg forced the spirit to his knees. The pressure built again, like the feeling of his nose being broken, but now slow and sustained across his skull.

"We need to run," Radek said.

"One sec," Ryan replied. He grunted and squeezed harder. Zef heard his skull crack before the world went dark and everything ceased to be.

Chapter 1
Prey

Shane stared up at the sun, one hand shielding his eyes, as he watched vultures circling a spot several miles away. They had found the bodies of the latest group of Reapers. Even a forest full of the dead couldn't keep vultures from a meal.

"Eat."

The big, hairy ghost called Oleg the Brute sat on a tombstone to Shane's left. Shane had never seen anything like him, living or dead. Nearly seven feet tall and hairy enough to be mistaken for a sasquatch, Oleg was pure muscle and madness.

Oleg spoke modern English well for a man born when Olde English was still common, as well as at least a dozen other languages, all of which he'd picked up after his death.

"Iron Tournament," the monster had explained.

He had been a champion of a European branch of the Iron Tournament and had toured much of the continent for years, fighting other competitors for the entertainment of the rich.

Shane could only imagine what would have happened if Oleg had been stateside when he was forced into the Tournament. The ghost was powerful and terrifying, but he was also not at all what Shane had expected.

"Killed too much," the ghost had told him not long after they met. "Done now."

Now he was free, or as free as a ghost could be. His haunted item was supposed to have been taken to Vakovia and laid to rest there. It was to be his reward for years of fighting. A chance at peace. There was a bit of a hiccup along the way, but Shane had rectified that after they met. And now, Oleg was concerned with Shane's eating habits.

"Later," Shane assured the spirit.

They had found supplies at a nearby village, enough to ensure he wouldn't starve. It was more than he had expected, but the kindness of Vakovians was surprising, even in the direst of circumstances.

"You think Oleg skipped food?" the big ghost asked. He flexed his arms, showing off biceps that rivaled the size of Shane's head, and laughing a deep, baritone laugh.

"I think Oleg ate people," Radek suggested. Oleg laughed louder, and the smaller man smirked.

Radek Dorn was once a Czech paratrooper. He had landed in a forest during a skirmish near the end of the Second World War. His chute was caught in the branches, and before he could free himself, enemy soldiers found him hanging there and slit his throat. They left his corpse hanging until it rotted out of the harness. Later, his spirit ended up in the city of Mostava.

Shane had been in the Vakovian wilderness for weeks since fleeing the Reaper's reinforcements in Seeburg. No city was safe for him, and even midsized towns posed too great a risk. When he passed through villages, he stayed out of sight as much as he could, only sneaking in to steal supplies when necessary.

It had been far too long since Shane had smoked a proper cigarette. Not only did that annoy him, it annoyed him how much it annoyed him. Men were trying to kill him and had relentlessly hunted him for weeks, but not being able to have a good cigarette was what stuck with him the most. None of the Reapers he'd fought had packs on them. One had a vape, which Shane refused to even try. The last chance he'd had to buy any was in the city of Mostava with Oleg, and those had long since run out. They weren't even a good brand.

Reapers had come to Vakovia by the dozens. Shane did not know how large the company was, but a Marine company was typically three platoons. That was two hundred forty-three Marines. If he was up against that many Reapers, then even with Oleg and Radek on his side, it would only be a matter of time.

Whoever was running the Reapers in the wake of Colonel Copland's death had not strategized well. They had sent Reapers into the wild after Shane in low numbers before all reinforcements had arrived. The piecemeal, staggered approach meant they could never move with enough force and enough firepower to take him on. By the time they had enough soldiers in Vakovia, Shane had long since vanished from their radar. He was dug in, and he had no intention of letting them find him.

Even with numbers, Vakovia was a large place full of empty spaces, ruins of a country that once was, and a population greatly disinterested in helping soldiers to find and kill a man. It was also a country full of the dead.

Shane spoke enough languages of the region to communicate with nearly everyone he came across. He did not fit in, but the locals could see he was on the run from what, to them, was the same corrupt military that tried to assassinate the man they wanted to be President. That was enough to make Shane one of them. Against the odds, he was succeeding.

"They send more men," Oleg pointed out, seeing the vultures.

"Yeah," Shane agreed.

They would send more. He would need to leave soon and find a new temporary base of operations. He liked where he was but, to be fair, he would have preferred being home in Nashua. He needed to get out of the damn country.

Every border crossing out of Vakovia was monitored. They had Shane's picture, and he was wanted for his involvement in the Seeburg incident.

Peter Zemba, the man branded a terrorist leader, had released a video of Copland's attack in the city. Copland and the Reapers, American military contractors working on behalf of President Janosik, were on full display killing multiple civilians in the marketplace in their attempt to take out Shane and Zemba.

International pressure had come down like a hammer on Janosik to justify the use of outside military forces to take out a supposed terrorist threat when the evidence showed a planned and staged slaughter of unarmed Vakovian citizens. It was ugly, and it cast light on the upcoming election that Janosik wanted to avoid.

The people of Vakovia might get a silver lining out of everything, but Shane was caught in the middle. The government wanted him dead, and by extension, that meant the Vakovian military and police. With the rest of Reaper Company included, it seemed like everyone with access to a gun in the country had their sights set on him.

There was an outside command structure to the Reapers, something far bigger than Copland. Shane was in no position to know what their plans were or who was executing them. Janosik was not the driving power; he was just a client.

"You could try Budapest again," Radek suggested.

Shane shook his head. The Hungarian border was heavily patrolled and monitored. There was no safe way to the other side, nor would there be any time soon. Plus, it was all the way back to the south, and he had no desire to double back where he had already been.

"Have to deal with this here," Shane said. "Now."

"Now?" Oleg asked.

"Soon," Shane corrected.

He'd been working on it for too long already, but if he wanted to stay alive, he needed to be smarter and more patient than the Reapers. He had been directed to a suitable spot in the remote north where he could lie low, fight when he needed to, and keep out of sight. It wouldn't last long, of course. The dead Reapers would attract more. They'd scour the area and force him into hiding until they left.

Once the Reapers left a zone, Shane was good for about a week of freedom. Then they'd double back. Eventually, he'd have to run again, or risk being discovered. There were no other options.

The cemetery no longer had a name or even any gates. It was half reclaimed by nature. Men in the nearby village called it the Cemetery of St. Jude Thaddeus. Shane took it as a good omen, not that he believed in such things. When he was directed there by others while he was still much farther south, they hadn't mentioned a name or much of anything. Just that he was needed there to fight, and he was offered assistance in escaping the Reapers in exchange.

The church, St. Jude's, was half rubble, with crumbling stone and decaying timbers. It was not suitable for cover, but it hid a secret. Through the floor below the southern transept was a secret passage that led to an ossuary. Someone had told Shane it was a kingdom of bones. He hadn't believed them at first.

Tunnels below the building were covered in bones from floor to ceiling. Skulls lined the walls by the thousands alongside ribs, spines, femurs, tibias, pelvic bones, and hands. It rivaled anything in Paris for scale, and it was all hidden away under a church no one knew existed.

"We will take cover?" Radek asked. "Wait them out?"

Shane nodded. His pattern had been to run. The Reapers would expect him to flee the area. They might even be anticipating it. Farther north was the likeliest place to go; it's where he would have fled if he were leaving. Because of that, it was precisely where he had no intention of going. If it seemed smart to him, it would seem smart to the enemy.

Reapers would likely cover the north in greater force, with smaller units to the east and west. South was no longer an option, with too much open land and Vakovian military patrols. He would continue to be where no one expected him. He'd stay alive, day by day.

"Let them run ragged in the mountains and freeze their asses," Shane said, nodding north. The snow-capped peaks were just barely visible from the graveyard. If he got past those, he'd potentially make it to Poland, and they didn't want that. Shane was leading them north in the hopes they'd assume that was his plan.

"They won't send all their forces to freeze," Radek pointed out. "They will be back."

"I know," Shane said.

Other spirits wandered the cemetery with them, sometimes stopping nearby as though they wished to join a conversation, though none spoke.

"They're the ghosts of ghosts," Radek once said of them. Lost even to him and Oleg. Many of them were bound to the ossuary, their bones having been gathered over centuries from the forests and fields and placed there to honor them.

"When you are bones, you look just like your enemy," Oleg pointed out. The ossuary did not care what side the dead fought on. They were all equal in death, and all were welcome to become a part of the temple of bone.

"We should do a supply check," Shane said, standing up. He did not know how long it would be until someone came to hunt down the fallen Reapers, but it would not be long. Maybe they'd send a chopper, or maybe SUVs over land. Either way, they would come.

Shane and the ghosts had been gathering supplies in the ossuary. They stripped the Reapers of everything they carried except electronics, so they couldn't be tracked. Guns, knives, body armor, matches, lighters, even shoelaces and belts. Anything that could be used in a pinch to set a trap or save Shane's life for another day.

Gasoline was siphoned from vehicles, as were any useful tools like tire irons, jumper cables, and first-aid kits. The bone cathedral had enough gear to outfit an entirely new squad.

Shane headed toward the ossuary entrance, moving through the rubble of the old church to the trap door concealed beneath a collapsed beam. He shifted a second beam and lifted the door beneath it. Oleg waited above to shift the beam back as Shane headed down the stairs and into the dark.

He used a match to light a small lantern at the bottom of the stairs and took out the knife from his belt, etching a notch into the stair post.

"Six weeks to the day," he said, looking at the assembled marks in the wood.

"Could be worse," Radek told him from the dark.

"Could be." Shane turned around and raised the lantern.

Shadows danced across the faces of a hundred skulls in the little vestibule at the base of the steps. Radek and Oleg waited at the entrance to the hallway that led to the depths of the ossuary.

"Six weeks," he said again as he followed them into the dark. Something scraped at the top of the stairs behind him, and he tensed, turning around in time to see three objects clatter down to the floor.

"Grenades!" he yelled, ducking into the hall with the ghosts.

CHAPTER 2
Six Weeks Ago

Two helicopters approached in the distance. The Reapers were coming, and Shane had little time to escape. He left the corpse of Colonel Copland and ran down the narrow passage between buildings, putting as much distance between himself and the helicopters as he could.

The first chopper landed to the north, cutting off Shane's access to his car. If the others hadn't found it before they arrived, these new Reapers certainly would. He would need an alternative escape route.

There was no way he could take on such a large number of reinforcements on his own. He was outmanned and outgunned. He wasn't sure he could even take on a single soldier or ghost in the condition he was in. He had one option.

Everyone in Seeburg was distracted running to or from the chaos. No one had time to pay attention to a single man who seemed to be doing the same. Shane ran to the town's eastern border and escaped to the open country beyond.

The second helicopter landed just as Shane left the town behind. The land beyond Seeburg was mostly scrub with the odd handful of trees here and there. Bushes, about chest height, provided the only cover as they dotted the landscape far and wide.

Shane ran from the town. He remembered the map, now stranded in his car, and had a vague sense of the world around him. There was a border crossing relatively close to the town. He might be able to get into Hungary if he was quick enough.

Once the Reapers realized he was gone from Seeburg, the border would be one of the first places they'd go to find him. He needed to be faster.

He ran as fast as his legs would carry him, darting from tree to shrub to tree, zigzagging through the desolate Vakovia countryside.

It had seemed like a way out was in his grasp. He should have known better than to expect it would be as simple as just getting rid of Copland and his spectral asset. Reaper Company was bigger than Shane had guessed, and Silvershore, the name of the contracting company they ran in Ravjek, was merely home to a single squad.

The helicopters were King Stallions, each able to carry close to forty Marines. They wouldn't have used two if they didn't need to. Copland sent for reinforcements in great numbers.

Shane ran until Seeburg was no longer visible and then slowed his pace. He was still making good time, but he couldn't push too hard. He had no food, no water, and no concrete idea of how far he needed to travel, or what awaited him when he found the border.

If Copland had alerted the locals, then the border would be a moot point. He still needed to try. It would be a lot easier to make his way home from Hungary than it would from Vakovia.

Hours passed. Shane had slowed to a walk, a comfortable pace he could maintain for many hours. He had passed no towns and seen no sign of life on his journey besides some birds of prey and some martens.

Ghosts dotted the landscape here and there, but none could help him. Some spoke dialects he had never encountered. Others were unable to hold coherent conversations and spoke to Shane as if he were an old friend or family member from decades in the past.

When he stumbled upon an old dirt road, he almost didn't notice it until he was standing in the middle of it. Nothing more than a flattened path of earth that stretched north to south, it bore no signs, and a close inspection suggested that no one had driven down it in weeks or even months.

It was the only thing Shane had seen since leaving Seeburg that suggested the living had ever been anywhere in the area. It was also pointed in the right direction.

Shane followed the road south, hoping to find a sign of the border. Based on his recollection of the map, he was certain the walk should have taken him to within a few miles of it.

The sun had already crossed the sky, and the day was fading into the evening when the distant sound of engines broke through the silence. Shane kept low and left the road, waiting for what sounded like an approaching vehicle. Soon, he realized it was not on the road behind him but farther east and approaching at an angle.

A ramshackle pickup truck, some relic of the eighties, rattled down another road heading in the same basic direction Shane was walking. He wished he had his binoculars to see what it was and where it was going, but it didn't look like military, neither Reapers nor Vakovian.

He jogged alongside the road for a distance, keeping out of sight as best as he could. The road he was on soon merged into a second road, the one on which he'd seen the truck. This one bore signs of more use in both directions, lined on either side with gravel and bearing the vestiges of numerous tire tracks in the dust and dried mud.

Shane followed the new road at a safe distance, once again sticking to shrubs and trees for cover. Several cars and trucks passed heading both south and north as he walked. Nothing came close to resembling the black SUVs that the Reaper Company drove in Ravjek. Instead, old trucks, vans, and rusted-out beaters built in the former Soviet Union rattled along carrying what looked like farmers and laborers going about their business.

Half an hour passed, and Shane ducked low again, taking cover in the underbrush as a small caravan of people on foot appeared on the road heading north. They pulled carts and wagons and had a donkey pulling the largest of them. About a dozen men and women carried enormous packs of goods on their backs or in the carts.

When the people passed, Shane could see the first hints of the border ahead of him. The road was blocked by a small gate between two buildings on either side and some fenced property.

The closer Shane got, the more he could see. A border station, a pair of outbuildings, and a fenced yard containing a few dozen people next to the main road. There was a second station and a second gate about fifty yards from the first. The nearest was monitored by the Vakovian military, but the second gate was manned by soldiers in a different uniform. Hungarian, Shane thought. He'd found what he was looking for, he just needed to get past two sets of guards. How hard could it be?

A handful of ghosts milled about the crossing as well, different from those he'd seen in the open country. These were not peasants or victims of ancient wars. Several had clear gunshot wounds to the head. These were spirits who had not made it across the border.

A fence extended east and west across the landscape, marking the official border between the countries. It was tall and foreboding with razor wire, but Shane couldn't help thinking anyone with bolt cutters would have been able to cross wherever they liked. Unfortunately, he had none.

A handful of people were at the border looking to cross. Shane made his way closer, as casual and unassuming as anyone else. Others were on foot, and there was a third, paved road that headed west along the border on which most of the traffic was moving. There was not an abundance of people waiting to cross, but it was far from the empty, forgotten crossing Shane had expected to find.

Officials checked papers on both sides, holding cars and more caravans on foot at the closed gates. People milled around listlessly in the pen to the left of the Vakovian border station while others sat against the fence and slept. It looked like a holding facility, probably for those detained for not having the right paperwork, or maybe with outstanding warrants.

As Shane approached, he could see another of the open-air pens, this one filled with women. There were probably close to a hundred people being detained.

Perhaps two dozen people on foot waited behind a van to cross into Hungary. Some sat in the patchy grass, others smoked and talked and kicked stones around restlessly. Shane joined the crowd, just another traveler, and took stock of the location. Security cameras were mounted on fences, on the border station roof, and on a handful of poles to get full coverage of the area. He'd already been caught on camera but had no interest in drawing attention.

He made his way to a ghost standing near the edge of the fence. He looked like he had once been a middle-aged man, of average height and looks, but with a hole through the center of his forehead trickling a glistening stream of blood into his left eye.

"They letting people through here?" Shane asked, leaning on the fence, and pulling a cigarette from his pocket.

The ghost looked at him and blinked, smearing the blood in his eye.

"You're talking to me?" the spirit answered. Shane nodded and then gestured to the holding pens.

"Looks like a lot of people are getting pulled out."

"Bad papers," the ghost said. "Most from Hungary trying to get in; some from here not allowed to leave. Vakovia does not welcome many outsiders."

"But getting into Hungary is easier?"

The ghost looked at Shane suspiciously.

"No. It's not," he said. "You are American?"

Shane nodded and exhaled a puff of smoke.

"On foot. Dirty. Bruised," the ghost said, gesturing to Shane's face. "You have a passport?"

Shane shook his head, and the ghost laughed bitterly.

"No. You will not cross. If the police are looking for you, they will have your face. Trust me, American. I would leave while you still can."

"Not a lot of other choices," Shane pointed out. He knew the cross would be a risk, but he needed to get out of Vakovia, and there were no other towns or crossings for miles.

The van was allowed to cross the border, and the group of people on foot got to their feet, snagging their belongings, and heading toward the gate to make their way into Hungary.

Shane nodded to the ghost and quickly joined the group of travelers, casually adding himself to the back of the pack so he blended in without seeming obtrusive to those who didn't recognize him.

Vakovian officials stopped the group, and Shane waited to see how things would play out. People held out papers and passports and talked over one another. There were only two guards on the Vakovian side, and they were only glancing at what those leaving the country had to offer, more concerned with those trying to come in from Hungary than those leaving.

The group was waved past the first gate. No one even looked in Shane's direction. He passed the border station and stayed with the pack as they made their way to the Hungarian gate where the van was still waiting for its final okay.

"You!"

The Hungarians had not yet finished with the van when the single word was yelled out from behind, on the Vakovian side. Some of the people with Shane turned to look back. It was a man's voice, loud and authoritative.

"Turn around," the voice said, closer now. Shane felt his chest tighten and could see some of the others looking at him. He turned and looked back.

A third Vakovian border patrol officer stepped out of the border station and was looking right at Shane. He approached with his rifle at the ready.

"You are Shane Ryan," the man said, raising his rifle. The people around him screamed and moved away, leaving Shane alone. The

Hungarian guards and the other Vakovians were alerted by the screams and now had weapons drawn as well, all on Shane. He raised his hands slowly.

"You are under arrest," the first officer said, circling Shane and pressing the barrel of his rifle to the back of his head. "Move."

CHAPTER 3
NO WAY OUT

"I told you."

The ghost was outside the holding pen, smirking at Shane.

"You told me," Shane agreed.

There were about twenty-five men in the fenced-in area with him. Like them, Shane had been stripped of the few belongings he'd had, including his cigarettes. One of the Vakovian guards was now smoking them. They missed the lighter he'd stashed in his boot while he waited to be processed, but he had nothing else of value on him.

"What happens now?" he asked.

The ghost shrugged.

"You stay until the truck comes."

"When does the truck come?"

"Today, tomorrow, whenever."

Shane looked around. There were no washrooms in the pen, no access to water, and he had strong doubts that the guards were cooking meals in their small office.

"You think it's unjust, hmm?" the ghost asked, watching Shane.

"That's one way to put it."

"Here's another," the ghost said, pointing to the hole in his head.

Shane paced the length of the pen several times. There were no specific weaknesses, no blind spots, and no obvious points from which he could escape. Only four Vakovian border agents were working, however, and the crowd of detainees was considerably larger. There was potential for a distraction if he timed things right. But he needed the pen unlocked, and that meant waiting for the right opportunity.

"I would not try to escape," the ghost said, catching Shane on his third circuit around the perimeter. He gestured to the hole in his head once more, and Shane grunted. He would have to remember to duck on his way out.

The distant sound of a helicopter grew louder as a dark speck on the horizon from the direction of Seeburg came into view. Shane watched the transport helicopter approach and then land a short distance from the road.

The sun had nearly set, but the helicopter's lights lit up the area like a small stadium. Lights on poles around the outdoor pen had also come on, fending off the impending darkness.

Shane watched the doors to the helicopter open and a half dozen men get out. If the black tactical gear and firepower didn't give them away, the group of ghosts that came from the helicopter with them did. Spectral assets for every man. Reaper Company had arrived.

Shane didn't know the man leading the group. He wore the same gear as the rest but had a rank insignia on his shoulder. Reaper Company was not official military, but they did like to play by some of the old rules. The man was a captain, a significant drop in rank from Copland, and likely not the head of the totem pole for the Reapers in Vakovia.

The captain approached the Vakovians while the other Reapers spread out in defensive positions, their rifles resting but ready. Most of the spectral assets stayed with their partners, but the spirit partnered with the captain appeared a moment after the ranking officer disappeared into the border station.

Milk-white eyes set into a desiccated face scanned the crowd in the pen before settling on Shane. The ghost was tall and willowy and bent to his left as though every bone in his body was curved just slightly. Even his skull seemed warped. His skin was mottled by dark, angry-looking bruises.

"There you are," the ghost whispered. His voice was harsh like his throat was too sore to speak louder or more clearly.

"Here I am," Shane replied.

The others in the pen could not see the spirits. They watched Shane warily, talking to himself in English as he seemed to be doing. The ghost ignored them, focusing only on Shane as he grinned, showing yellowed teeth.

"Heard you're a real bad hombre," he said. "You took on Dell back in Seeburg is what I heard."

"Well, aren't you all gossipy little hens," Shane replied.

The ghost drifted into the pen, circling Shane.

"How long do you think until they're finished in there?" the ghost asked, nodding to the office.

"You got somewhere else to go?"

"Just thinking… if I kill you now, maybe they'll all just think it was one of these suckers stuck in the cage with you. Just a dispute between prisoners. You're dead, we all go home."

"Think your boss won't take kindly to you breaking protocol," Shane said.

The ghost's grin widened.

"Who's gonna tell him?"

Shane shook his head as the ghost continued to circle him like a predator inspecting its prey.

"That's just a lack of discipline," he told the ghost. "Disregarding orders and acting alone? You're a piss-poor soldier."

"I never signed up to be a soldier. Just to kill people like you."

"You've never killed anyone like me," Shane said. The spirit stopped with his back to the office, as far from the view of the other Reapers and their spectral assets as he could get. "And you never will."

The ghost came at him, moving swiftly despite his twisted shape. He went for Shane's throat, arms extended like some horror movie Frankenstein, and a snarl on his bruised and battered face. No finesse.

Shane caught the ghost by the wrist and then fell back, letting momentum carry them to the ground as he put a foot up and planted it into the ghost's gut.

The ghost flipped, a hoarse cry of surprise escaping his lips before he landed hard on the dirt next to the fence. Shane spun and rolled on top of the spectral form, planting a fist firmly in the middle of his face.

The other detainees murmured in confusion, watching Shane writhe and struggle with nothing. He did not like to make a scene, but desperate times called for quick thinking. There wasn't time to worry about the consequences.

Shane slammed an elbow into the ghost's jaw, shattering the bone, and preventing him from calling out. With one hand holding the spirit's neck, he pressed down on the already warped skull.

Bone crunched, and the ghost's body exploded with a violent burst. The fence buckled outward as Shane was thrown back toward the crowd of detainees.

"They're trying to kill us," he shouted in Hungarian as he came to a rest at the feet of a man in a dark jacket.

Murmurs and then shouts ran through the crowd. The fence began to collapse, and a trio of men rushed toward it, pushing it over. Soon, the others joined, seeing their chance for escape and fearing that the Reapers had used some kind of weapon against them.

The Reapers near the chopper raised their rifles, and the scene exploded in chaos. The Hungarian border officers drew on the Reapers, as did the Vakovians. People shouted in multiple languages as the detainees took the fence down and ran.

Screams filled the air, orders were shouted, and men fled in all directions. Shane stormed across the fence, joining the others and fleeing into the Vakovian countryside. Shots were fired from behind, answered by others. Soon, an entire firefight broke out between the three forces.

Some shots were directed at the escapees. Shane watched a man ahead of him felled by a bullet through the leg. More shots rang out, and shouts for a ceasefire were ignored on all sides.

Shane ran with a dozen men toward a scraggly outcropping of trees a few hundred yards away.

"You want to go there," a familiar voice said.

The ghost with the hole in his head paced Shane across the countryside. Some of the escapees ran for the road and others headed northwest. The largest group, Shane's group, aimed for the trees. The ghost, however, was pointing dead west, far to the right of the visible cover of the woods.

"What's there?"

"River," the ghost said.

Shane had endured an impromptu swim in Vakovia once already, but it had gotten him to safety.

The helicopter engine started up in the distance, and Shane redoubled his efforts. He broke from the pack of panicking men, leaving them to their small forest destination as he stayed in the scrub-filled countryside, trusting the ghost's guidance.

"Where does the river go?" he asked.

"North," the ghost replied. It was not the best answer, but it would do.

Flashes of the red and purple sky reflected off the water as it came into view. He could hear the rush of it blending with the sound of the helicopter to create a flurry of white noise.

The setting sun was already beyond the horizon. The Reapers probably had night vision at their disposal, but if Shane could get into the water, it would limit their ability to find him.

His breath came in strained gasps, and he pushed as hard as he could. The helicopter was nearly overhead. A spotlight hit the men running for the woods off to Shane's left, and shots rang out as it began to descend. Shane ignored it all. He was at the river.

"You should—" the ghost began. The rest of his advice was lost as Shane leaped into the water without pause. He guessed the river was close to two hundred feet wide where he entered, and the current was swift and harsh.

He was swept away quickly as he swam from the shore, allowing the water to drag him along as he avoided snags that were close to land. He was pulled along between rocks and over dips as the speed increased.

"Stay near the shore," the ghost finished, appearing in the water with him. White froth rose and swamped them as Shane was spun around and dunked. His shoulder hit a rock, and he groaned, inadvertently swallowing a mouthful of water before he surfaced and spit out what he could.

The ghost spoke again, but his advice was washed out by the sound of the water rushing around more rocks as the rapids picked up speed. It was all Shane could do to stay above and keep breathing. The sound of the helicopter was gone, and the last vestiges of the sun's rays vanished from the horizon, plunging the river into darkness. He was being dragged downstream through inky black water with no idea of where he was headed.

Shane was alone, the ghost no longer following. He guessed they had passed the limits of the ghost's reach, and it was forced to return to the border where it had started. Rocks appeared like phantoms and battered him. He began to regret his decision to swim away from the shore, but he needed the distance. He still needed it. If he went to shore now, the helicopter would find him in minutes.

He swam with the current, did his best to keep his head above water, and tried to move at an angle against the current. He did everything to stop himself from going under every time the water swirled around another boulder or felled tree, but it was no use.

Again and again, Shane found himself dunked below the surface and then bobbing up again, getting pounded against the stones and detritus. At one point, he tried to shift toward the western shoreline and only succeeded in spinning himself backward, making it impossible to see where he was going.

Shane cursed, taking more water in his mouth, and rolling over in the river in time to see a large, stump-shaped boulder rush toward him. He kicked and pushed, but there was not enough time to avoid it.

His head hit the stone with an ugly crunch, and he felt pain run straight down his spine for only a moment. It rattled his teeth and made it feel like his entire skull had split.

Shane's eyes rolled back, and the world went icy cold.

Chapter 4
The Apple Man

"You're not dead."

The voice was Russian. Shane opened his eyes and looked up. He was cold and wet, but he was, as observed, not dead.

A one-eyed ghost looked down at him, dressed in a Russian uniform that must have come from sometime around the Revolution. He had been stabbed in the face, and his eye plucked free. His hat sat off-kilter on the other side of his head.

"Where am I?" Shane asked in Russian.

"In the river," the ghost answered.

Shane sat up awkwardly, and the world spun and tossed. He felt like he was falling. Pain ran through his head, and he reached up to gingerly touch a cut on his scalp.

He was on a muddy bank under heavy tree cover. The land was much more verdant than it had been where he entered the river, and the pace of the water had slowed to a crawl.

There were tears in his clothes, and he was bleeding in a half-dozen places. But he was most definitely not dead.

"They're looking for you," the Russian said.

"Who?" Shane asked, touching the wound on his head again. He felt like he'd given himself a concussion but couldn't tell if it required stitches.

"In the sky," the ghost said, gesturing up. "What do you call that flying machine?"

"Helicopter," Shane said.

"Helicopter," the ghost repeated. "It flies up and down. Must be looking for something. Maybe you."

"Maybe me," Shane agreed. The tree cover was dense enough above him that if someone had flown by, he could have easily been missed.

"I need to get out of here."

"Good idea," the Russian agreed. "You need a doctor."

"Know any?" Shane asked, slowly getting to his feet. Moving made him feel nauseated, and everything was spinning. He used a tree to steady himself and then paused to take a few calming breaths before he opened his eyes.

"Doctor in town," the Russian said, pointing at nothing in specific.

"What town?"

"Town there. Zevna," he said, pointing again at nothing but trees.

Shane tried to remember the map but could not recall seeing a Zevna listed. He climbed up the bank away from the river and got onto dry ground in a sparse forest. Sunlight streamed through the spaces between the trees and dense thickets of ferns, allowing wild raspberries and other plants to grow in the light.

"How far?" Shane asked.

"Quarter of a mile," the ghost answered.

Shane started walking, pushing through the dense foliage, and keeping an eye on the sky as he went for signs of the helicopter. His boots squished, and his clothes hung heavy, but the walk and the sun soon dried most of what he had to the point that it was no longer bothersome.

He was covered in filth, caked with river mud that had dried all over him, and assumed that his face must have matched with a healthy dose of bruises and scrapes to make him look like a crazed wild man from the forest.

As the ghost promised, a town was only a short distance. He saw faint wisps of smoke from chimneys as he drew closer and slowed his progress, taking cover and moving cautiously to get the lay of the land. The town was below him, down a slight incline into a valley. The elevation gave him a chance to get a good look at the place.

The town was little more than a village, home to maybe one hundred buildings. One road cut through the center while smaller streets bisected it at regular intervals to create a tiny, uneven grid.

Shane could see some shops along the main road, but very little looked more modern than the eighties. They did have a pizza place he could make out, thanks to the large sign. It was nestled on the main road next to a post office and what might have been a market. The biggest building in the town was a church in the middle of it.

Zevna was too large for the Reapers to ignore. If they were sweeping down the river, they would stop there eventually. But it was large enough to afford Shane a number of hiding places. If they planned to hunt him, he would make them work for it.

There was no obvious sign of the Reapers in town. None of the vehicles belonged to them, and he could not see the helicopter, but he was not yet willing to discount their presence.

Shane moved stealthily toward the edge of the town and came up through a property behind a small orchard growing a modest number of apple trees among overgrown grass at the southern edge of the place.

He weaved through the evenly planted trees, taking several apples and stashing them in his pockets. He reached a barn and stayed out of sight as he circled the place, glancing through windows and cracks in the boards for signs of life.

The sooner he got out of sight, the better, Shane thought. The fewer people who saw him, and the smaller impact he had on the town, the less likely the Reapers would be to find him. They were still too close for him to take any chances. He would lie low for a time, find a doctor, and then leave.

A rusty lock and chain held the barn door closed, but it was loose enough for him to push in one side of the double doors and slip inside. The interior was dusty and dim with only a handful of small, dirty windows and cracks in the wood to let in light.

Wooden baskets and bushels were piled high along the back wall, half of them tumbled over and caked in layers of dust. A massive metal vat, some kind of cistern or fermentation tank, that looked like it came from a century in the past, filled the bulk of the room. It looked as though no one had been in the barn for ages.

The state of the orchard outside was a little rough. No one had trimmed the weeds in some time, but the apples seemed to be taking care of themselves. He wondered if the farmers had abandoned the place or if they had died. No one else had stepped up to care for it, that much was clear.

Shane crept through the barn, searching for potential weapons or resources. Midway through the barn, he found a handle attached to a wooden floor plank. There was a cellar.

The hinges creaked as Shane lifted the door. The cellar was beyond the reach of the light. He pulled his Zippo from where he'd stashed it at the border station and tried to light it, but river water had saturated it. He couldn't get a spark.

Undeterred, Shane continued down a sturdy, wooden ladder to the cellar, easing the door shut after him. He waited at the bottom of the steps while his eyes adjusted, the faintest hints of light creeping through the floorboards above and illuminating little more than shapes and a general outline of the space.

Shelves made of spare barn board lined the walls, holding up large, dusty jugs. Shane retrieved one and worked out a cork, smelling the contents and wincing. It might have once been cider, but it was vinegar now, sharp to the nose and reeking of fermented apple. He recorked the jug and placed it back on the shelf.

The air was cool in the cellar, as it was all over the north of Vakovia. Stacks of old burlap sat on a crate near the shelves, and Shane pulled some free, unfolding them to check their condition. It was rough and old and stiff, but it would serve as impromptu bedding for a day or two.

He needed to throw the Reapers off, and he could not keep running. Holing up in the cellar would give him time to heal, rest, and plan. The Reapers would hopefully be convinced they'd missed him and would continue spreading out, spending less time focusing on where he was and more on where they hoped to find him.

Shane sat on a pile of burlap and leaned his back against a crate. He ate one of the apples he'd taken from the orchard. The fruit was juicy and a good mix of sour and sweet. He hadn't eaten in more than a day, and it was a welcome treat after what he'd been through.

His head throbbed, and his muscles ached. Shane had only been conscious for a short time, but the dimly lit cellar was lulling him to sleep. He knew he should have resisted, if for no other reason than his head injury needed to be seen to, but he couldn't bring himself to care. He closed his eyes and was asleep in seconds.

The smell of rotten apples and rancid meat woke Shane up. It filled his nostrils in a cloying way, overly sweet and impossible to ignore. His eyes snapped open, and he sat upright. The room was as dim as it had been when he fell asleep, only something had changed.

The steps to the barn had vanished, as had some of the walls. The space had expanded. It was no longer a tiny storage room for cider but a warehouse, a full and seemingly boundless basement.

Shane exhaled as though he could force the smell from his nose. A heavier chill filled the room, and he was not surprised. Something dead was in the cellar with him. Someone dead.

"I just stopped here to rest for a bit," he said to the cellar. "I'll be out of your hair in a couple of days."

The light that filtered through the cracks above began to wane, the tiny beams thinning out even smaller as the angle changed. The smell of rotten apples grew stronger, to the point that Shane felt his eyes watering.

He got to his feet and looked for any sign of movement. The spirit was well hidden in the shadows and had not made a sound, but the illusion it constructed was as solid as anything Shane had seen. The smell was pungent enough that he could taste vinegar at the back of his throat.

The lights between slats in the floorboards above his head continued to thin out until they winked from existence. They vanished one by one until only a single, pencil-thick beam of dim, gray light fell between two boards where Shane stood.

Something in the dark moved. A slow, deliberate scrape like something heavy dragging across the floor. Shane waited, his eyes poised on the darkness where the sound seemed to have originated from.

A second scrape, closer this time, was followed by a muffled thud. Scrape and thud, scrape and thud, each a little louder than the one before.

Shane did not move, either to approach the sound or to flee. He waited. The smell grew stronger, and a new sound rose in the darkness. Just as each scrape began there was a wet groan, like someone gargling with a mouth too full of liquid. The sloppy squelching preceded new bursts of the stench as though blasting the rancid odor toward Shane through the dark.

A figure appeared in the scant light ahead of him. It was a man, limping on a shattered, bent foot. The thump came as his good foot hit the ground; the scrape as he dragged the second, shattered limb behind.

The tiny beam of light fell on the spirit's face. His flesh was stained a rich, dark brown and was wrinkled profusely, not from age but from moisture. Flesh glistened and dripped as it hung loosely from the ghost's skull. His face seemed in the process of sliding off, the skin too loose and sodden to stay on the bone any longer.

His eyelids hung heavy, half covering stained and ugly yellow eyes. When he moved, he groaned and mouthfuls of thick, rancid liquid bubbled out and spilled down his saturated coveralls. The stench of rancid apple was as strong as it would get.

The ghost must have drowned in the vat of cider in the barn. The acid and tannins stained and all but destroyed the flesh in a way Shane had never seen.

Words muffled by bubbling, fermented cider gurgled from the ghost's throat, but Shane could understand none of it, not even what language it was.

"If you're trying to tell me something, you're going to need to clear your throat," he told the spirit.

The ghost gurgled again, and his throat bulged obscenely, causing the hanging flesh to expand and smooth the wrinkles. A gout of viscous, chunky vomit erupted from his throat and splashed out across the floor with a loud splatter. Things moved in it, though they were hard to see in the darkness. Small, writhing creatures, struggling with their newfound freedom on the cellar floor.

"I just wanted to rest," Shane muttered.

The ghost raised a hand, stained flesh hanging limply from its fingers. It struggled forward.

CHAPTER 5
DOWN LOW

The last light winked from existence, and Shane was plunged into darkness. The gurgling and scraping went silent. The stench of festering flesh and rotten apples was so thick that it felt like a physical thing was trying to smother him.

Cold air swirled around him, and Shane gauged where the ghost had gone. The silence stretched on for too long and he waited, hands balled into fists, for the ghost to strike.

Fingers grasped Shane by the legs, and something pulled at the back of his shirt. He swung blindly and hit nothing as he fell back, landing in the pile of burlap. Light slashed through the dark, beams of it splitting the cracks in the floorboards but drifting back and forth as though the light source above was spinning and moving about the room.

The ghost was on top of Shane. It belched, and a torrent of thick, acidic vomit washed across his face. He could feel things squirming in it, wriggling across his face and under the collar of his shirt.

Disgust was overwhelmed by anger. The ghost leaned forward, its rancid jaws open and dripping. It leaned in to bite Shane's face, and Shane growled, raising a fist to meet the ghost and cut it off.

Shane's knuckles slammed into the ghost's mouth. Bloated, rotten gums gave with ease, and the creature's stained, brown teeth collapsed inward as Shane punched straight to the back of the ghost's throat.

They struggled on the cellar floor. The ghost's rotten hands first clutched Shane's neck and then switched to trying to remove his fist. Shane took hold of the ghost's head with his free hand, its flesh squishing in his grip, and forced his fist deeper.

Ghost flesh gave way like ultra-thick jelly. His fingers plunged through it, clawing for something more solid, until he struck bone. The ghost writhed and jerked like a rabid animal trying to escape, but Shane refused to give it quarter now. Exhaustion and anger clouded his mind. The ghost had picked the wrong time to start a fight.

Shane's fingers set upon something stronger than the rest of the unnatural spirit flesh. He closed his fist around it, a segment of bone no thicker than the handle of a baseball bat.

With a suppressed growl of strain, Shane lifted his legs and pushed against the ghost with his feet as he released the hand on the back of the thing's head. His grip inside the ghost's body was as tight as he could make it.

Bones snapped and flesh tore. Shane pulled the ghost's spine through his mouth, causing his neck to snap backward and his head to fall off. The ghost's body shuddered as the spine came free and then burst, rattling the bottles on the shelves and sending plumes of dust into the air.

Shane coughed, covering his face to breathe in as little as he could. The stench was gone, along with the filth, and he was dry and alone once more.

His head hurt less, and he could feel dry blood scabbed around it. He decided to wait it out rather than seek a doctor and risk exposing himself.

With sleep no longer an option, Shane scoured the cellar for anything useful. The Vakovians at the border had taken his iron rings, but he found a box of old nails, the same ones used to assemble the barnboard shelves. At just a few inches long, they fit easily between his fingers and would be better than nothing in a pinch if he had to make a fast escape from a spectral asset in the future.

A shelf below the stairs revealed itself to be full of bottles of apple wine. Shane took one back to his burlap bed and settled in once more. The smell was far less acidic than what had become of the cider, and even though it faintly reminded him of the ghost's stench, he was thirsty and without an abundance of options.

By the time night fell, his head was buzzing just enough to let him know he needed to stop drinking.

✸ ✸ ✸

It had to be afternoon, judging by the angle of the light. It was hard to tell through two sets of boards, but Shane did his best. He had finished the stolen apples and a bottle of apple wine. Not a living thing had encroached on the barn, and he hadn't heard anything come close outside, either.

Once, early in the day, he heard a helicopter pass in the distance, but it didn't stop or land anywhere within earshot. He crept up the stairs from the cellar and returned to the barn.

Patience was the name of the game. Shane waited at the cellar entrance, letting the seconds tick by. If anything heard him moving, it gave no sign. He lowered the door carefully and silently and made his way to the entrance.

From the door, he had a view of the road leading south out of Zevna. He sat and watched, hidden in shadows, observing who came and went.

The road through Zevna received significant traffic, more than Shane would have guessed based on other small towns he'd seen in Vakovia. Maybe its proximity to the Hungarian border crossing made it more of a hub of activity.

Cars came and went, hardly what he'd call rush hour by American standards, but enough to indicate people knew Zevna. The Reapers would be aware of it.

He saw a farmer leading a small herd of goats on foot, and some children leaving town to play soccer in parts unknown. A handful of pedestrians came close to the apple orchard, and an old man even walked up the property, dangerously close to the barn, to harvest apples, which he placed in a bag before heading back the way he'd come.

No one stirred in the old farmhouse, and no one came to the barn. The place was abandoned, as Shane had surmised.

Vakovian military vehicles rolled through town in the late afternoon. A trio of Jeeps, leaving to the south. Two of them kept moving, but one stopped. The driver and three others got out and split up. They were searching every property.

Shane made his way back to the cellar, holding some old wooden slats atop the door so they'd cover it as he dropped inside. He waited below in the dark for nearly twenty minutes before he heard the chain on the door rattle. The door creaked, and something thumped loudly.

Shane watched between the narrow cracks as a shadow appeared and one of the Vakovians wandered through the barn. Dust fell on Shane as the man walked across the floorboards. Shane could make out the weapon in his hands.

The Vakovian used his foot to kick some bushels and turned around again, heading back the way he came. The chain rattled, the door creaked, and he was gone. Shane could faintly hear the Jeep engines several minutes later. He was alone and safe, at least for a while.

Shane spent the rest of the day using a spool of thin, old wire along with the nails he'd found to fashion himself a set of poor man's iron knuckles, wrapping the wire around his fists and using the nails as spikes. If he hit a solid target hard enough, he'd probably hurt himself, but it was better than nothing, and it'd dispatch both ghosts and the living.

Shane crept from the barn after sunset and snagged a few more apples from the orchard to fill his pockets. He planned to head west and then north again, further distancing himself from Seeburg and the border.

He moved silently along the edge of the farmhouse to the front of the property. He planned to skirt around Zevna, but he hadn't even reached the road when he heard the staccato rumbling in the distance. A helicopter was on the way.

Shane cursed and waited at the side of the road under the cover of a tree for a handful of cars to pass. When the final set of taillights were gone, he ran across the street and into a field of green barley.

The tall grass reached his chest and whipped at his arms as he plowed through it, aiming for trees at the far end of the field. Whether it was a forest or a simple thicket, he couldn't say, but it would provide cover and keep him away from prying eyes.

Ghosts in the field murmured at his passing but he ignored them. The helicopter was closer, and a searchlight pierced the darkness like a pillar of white fire, scanning the world below as it approached.

The thunder of the blades filled the air and Shane dove for the ground, crawling forward to hide beneath the grass. His surroundings exploded with light as the searchlight passed over him and kept moving. The wind from the helicopter blades stirred the grass and pressed the stalks down on top of him, providing better cover, and in seconds, the light and the helicopter were gone, passing over the field and across the road to the orchard.

Shane sat up to watch the chopper move onward, entering the airspace over the town while the light scanned back and forth in a sweeping pattern.

The light was for the benefit of the living. The ghosts on board would have a keener sense of what hid in the dark.

Staying low, Shane continued toward the trees, keeping his eye on the helicopter and its searchlight as he moved. At some point, the helicopter fell below where he could see. Seconds later, the engine sounds geared down. They'd landed.

Shane ran. Grass whipped around him as he pumped his legs and navigated the uneven ground of the field. He kept going when he reached the tree line, weaving between the trunks of oak and walnut until he was positive that he was fully hidden from view.

He slowed his pace but continued to move, pausing only long enough to orient himself and listen. There were no sounds of the chopper taking off, and no sounds of pursuit. He kept going.

The woods began to thin out again, and Shane slowed his pace further. The forest was only a thin stretch, nothing robust enough to travel through for any great distance. As the trees grew farther and farther apart, he found himself in the empty countryside once more. The land looked like it had once been cultivated and farmed, but not for a generation or more. A field of tall grass and weeds, dotted with trees, waited for him.

He turned to look the way he had come and caught the faintest hint of movement. Something disappeared behind a tree.

Shane watched and waited. Whatever he had seen did not reappear. It had been a flicker, a barely registered blip in the dark of the forest. He had not even had enough time to determine what he saw, but his gut told him it was a ghost.

That spirits roamed the Vakovian countryside was not surprising, but he had not seen this one on his way through the woods. And it had not reemerged from behind the tree. That was something that happened when someone didn't intend to be seen in the first place.

He kept moving, leaving the small patch of woodland behind, and headed into the overgrown field. The grass here grew taller than Shane, and the flat leaves had a faint sandpaper quality that tugged at his arms and made a shushing sound as they scraped against him.

He was only several yards deep into the tall grass when he paused again to listen. The shushing sound kept on, even as he stayed still.

"You should run," a voice whispered from the darkness behind him, obscured by the wall of green stalks. "I like it when they run."

Chapter 6
In the Tall Grass

Grass parted as a shadow rushed forward, less a man than the shape of one. Shane pulled his hand from his pocket and took a swipe, his wire-and-nail iron knuckles held tightly in his fist. Before he could even focus on the spirit, the nails hit unliving flesh and forced the ghost back to its haunted item.

Shane turned and ran. They knew where he was now, and his time was short. He bolted through the long grass, feeling the rough, sandpaper blades lash at his exposed arms and face like a thousand paper cuts.

The thrum of helicopter blades returned behind him. He cursed and pushed as hard as he could. There was nowhere to go and nothing he could see beyond the endless wall of green grass and black sky above. If a forest waited, another river, a town, even a bald cliff face that would plunge him a hundred feet onto jagged rocks, he had no idea.

Light passed through the blades of grass as the helicopter approached. The spotlight scanned the field as it passed over the edge of the trees. The sound of the world was drowned out, leaving only the roar of the helicopter's engines and the repetitive beat of the whirling blades.

Shane would not stop. If they wanted him, they'd work for him. He ran, even as the light from the chopper fixed on him, lighting the grass as bright as the midday sun.

Something fell from the helicopter directly in his path, and he did not slow. The ghost, still little more than a shadow but with a vaguely recognizable face of a man, opened his mouth to say something. Shane punched him again without pause. Iron nails reacted to ghost flesh, and the spectral asset vanished.

A heartbeat later, the ghost dropped from the helicopter again. Shane plunged his hand back into his pocket and dropped the iron knuckles. This time, he met the ghost barehanded. No words were exchanged; he tackled the shadow, planting a shoulder into the spirit's gut.

They fell together in the grass. The fury of the wind created by the chopper's blades flattened the grass on top of them, obscuring them from the view of those above. Shane slammed a knee in the ghost's groin and then lifted the ghost's left leg, hyperextending it and forcing it down with all of his strength until he heard something pop.

The ghost screamed, much of the sound drowned out by the helicopter.

"You have no idea what's in store for you," the spirit growled, hooking an arm around Shane's neck and pulling him down so they were face to face.

"No?" Shane asked, clutching the ghost's head between his hands. "Do you have any idea what's in store for your buddies in that helicopter?"

The ghost's expression was nothing but confusion, if only for a moment. Shane squeezed the ghostly flesh with all his might until bone crushed. The ghost's half-formed shadowy body exploded and knocked Shane to the side. He lay there for a moment, staring up and watching as the helicopter lurched hard to the left.

The front end spun sharply downward until the helicopter was vertical, and then it kept spinning. Shane got back to his feet and ran in the opposite direction. The ghost's partner must have been the pilot. When the haunted item he carried burst, it either killed or grievously wounded him. Either way, he was no longer able to fly.

Flames lit up the night as the King Stallion's nearly 2,300-gallon fuel tank exploded. The blast scorched the field of grass and sent Shane flying forward as if he'd been hit by a truck.

Debris rained from the sky, flaming bits of rubble scattering like rain.

One of the massive rotor blades sailed through the air just feet from Shane, shearing through the grass like a high-powered scythe and cutting down several thin trees as if they were nothing.

Shane coughed and got to his hands and knees, catching his breath as the last remnants of the helicopter fell to the earth, setting smaller fires in dozens of spots throughout the field.

The force of the blast had flattened the grass all around, and when Shane stood, he could see a handful of spirits gathered around with several more joining from the darkness, all drawn to the excitement.

Shane watched them and assessed. They were not all local ghosts. One in the heart of the flaming wreckage was different from the others. A man with close-cropped hair and old army surplus fatigues. His eyes were fixed on Shane, and even at a distance, Shane could sense the ghost's hate. He was one of the spectral assets.

"Hell of a ride, huh?" Shane shouted, not sure if he could be heard over the fire.

The ghost said nothing as he ran then lunged for Shane's face. Shane deflected the attack and kicked the ghost's knee, knocking him to the ground.

The spirits in the field drew closer, watching the battle but neither speaking nor involving themselves. It reminded Shane of his time in the ghost city of Kogar, where the dead simply stood by and watched en masse.

Shane could feel the weariness of the past two days sapping his strength. His arms were sore, his head throbbed, and every blow he struck felt like a monumental achievement. The tank was nearly empty, and he could not keep going like this.

His opponent fought clumsily. The ghost's hand-to-hand skills were as unrefined as most spirits', unused to having to defend themselves as so many were. Ghosts spent too long being unseen and untouchable that they lost their ability to defend or strike with competency. It was Shane's saving grace.

Under the watchful eyes of a dozen silent spirits, Shane punched the spectral asset's face with his full weight behind it. Ghostly flesh and bone squelched and popped. The ghost burst and knocked Shane back. The assembled spirits were also thrust away, not as forcefully, but enough to make the nearest of them stumble.

Shane was on his back, staring up at a black sky and breathing heavily. He could have slept right there. He could have stopped fighting and given in so easily. Part of him wanted to.

A ghost came into his field of view, though, and he swore out loud. The spirit was of an elderly man, bald with a long, snow-white beard. His face was wrinkles upon wrinkles, and his eyes were unfocused.

He spoke a language Shane didn't recognize. There were hints of something Cyrillic, but it sounded like nothing he had heard before. Judging from the ghost's simple clothing made of rough fabric in a style as foreign as his words, Shane suspected the ghost was far older than most he'd met.

"I don't understand," Shane said, closing his eyes and breathing deeply. He was willing himself to stand, to get up and run again, but it was taking some time. The warmth from the nearby fire was comforting, and the bed of grass was softer than he expected.

"He asks if you are the man that kills the dead," a new voice asked.

Shane opened his eyes again. Another ghost stood with the old man. He was younger, and his clothes were more modern. Half of his face was torn away, maybe from an accident or an explosion based on the appearance.

"Ghosts aren't alive, so they can't be killed," Shane pointed out.

"But you are the man? From Ravjek? And Kogar?"

Slowly, and painfully, Shane got back to his feet. The spirits had formed a rough semicircle around him that made it seem like he was meant to address them with a speech he had no intention of giving. The old man's ghost and his translator stood in the center.

"I've been to those cities, yeah," Shane confirmed.

"You have fought the dead and destroyed them like you did this one. The old man says he has heard of you. Many of us have," the translator spirit said.

Shane looked over the spirits. Some looked like they could have died as recently as that week; others looked to be from decades or even centuries in the past.

"You've heard of me?"

"Nothing happens in Vakovia that the dead do not know," the translator said.

"Where I come from, most ghosts aren't as up to date on current events."

"Vakovia is a country of the dead, As you may have noticed."

The translator gestured to the others, and Shane nodded.

"I have."

"And you saw Kogar. You saw Ravjek and Seeburg and the lands between. The dead walk. And the dead talk."

Shane nodded, looking at the ancient spirit watching him.

"Like some kind of spiritual whisper network. You just play the telephone game across the countryside, one ghost to the next."

The reference was lost on the translator, but Shane waved it off.

"I need to get going," he told them. Whether he had become a minor celebrity to the spirits of Vakovia or not didn't mean much to him or his chances of survival. Reapers would come soon to find their fallen comrades.

The old spirit spoke, and the younger ghost translated, speaking over him.

"There was one like you in Vakovia, years ago. A hundred years plus dozens more. A man who talked to the dead and could tear them to pieces as though they were still living flesh," the translator said.

"Sounds like a great guy," Shane said.

"But since he died, there have been none," the translator continued. "Most do not know your kind exists. Or could exist."

Shane had not met many people who could interact with spirits as he did. Some could see them, and some could talk to them, but interacting was rare, and he knew it. It seemed that was true all over the world.

"The spirits of Vakovia are in harmony with the land," the translator continued. "Death has visited this place generation after generation. Those who can't resist its call cannot exist in the open."

"What the hell does that mean?" Shane asked.

"The dead who are violent," the translator clarified without the old man's help. "The... vengeful dead? They are not like us. They are shunned."

Shane grunted. Most of the spirits he had run across seemed friendly or at least docile. And the more violent ones, like the Apple Man, were hiding in places alone. He had not considered that was by design.

"So, you police your own," Shane said. The translator considered the words.

"Perhaps, yes. But..." he looked at the ancient spirit who pointed somewhere to the north and began to speak again.

"There is a place far from here," the translator continued. "There is one there who does not exist in peace. It is an abomination, but it has great strength. Those who have faced it have failed. If you go there, if you face this abomination, you will not fail."

Shane looked north and saw grass and fire from the helicopter. There was a lot of land between him and Vakovia's northern border.

"You want to put a hit on a ghost?"

Chapter 7
Overland

The dead of Vakovia had grown sick of death. Generations of war had bred contempt among those who did not survive. Vakovia's dead were unsettled and numerous, more so than anywhere Shane had seen. And the effect of all the mass death had been the opposite of what he expected.

Instead of being spirits of hate and anger, the ghosts of Vakovia longed for a simple peace with the land they occupied. They wanted to exist and be undisturbed. They wanted people to stop dying.

Ghosts that didn't follow the general consensus were not allowed to exist in the open and roam the world in which they once lived. They were forced underground, into tunnels and cellars and shadows. Or they were destroyed. It seemed like a reasonable system. Ghosts keeping other ghosts in check. Carl would have loved it.

"The spirit in the north is on sacred land. It is blasphemy for it to kill and mock the sanctity of life as it does," the translator explained.

"You learned this through your network?" Shane asked.

"Until there were none left to share the story. Destroyed by this spirit, we think. It is a blind spot for us now."

"And you know nothing about who the ghost is, why it kills, how, or anything like that?"

"No," the translator spirit explained. "Those details were never of interest."

"To you," Shane said. They could have made a world of difference to him.

"You are pursued by these men," the translator continued, gesturing to the flaming helicopter. "They pursued you in Kogar, and the dead helped you escape. They pursued you in Ravjek and Seeburg. Even at the Hungarian border. But we helped you."

Shane nodded. It wasn't hard to see where the ghost was going. He wanted a little postmortem quid pro quo. It was the only offer of aid Shane was likely to get any time soon, and it was probably the best one he could hope for.

"When you say *you* will help, you mean... the dead. All of Vakovia's dead," he said.

"All who wish for the same peace," the translator told him.

There were probably layers of meaning in that statement that Shane couldn't hope to unpack, but it didn't matter. He had seen what the dead of Kogar could do when they worked together. And he had seen the sheer numbers of dead across the countryside.

"What kind of help are we talking about?" Shane asked.

The old spirit started speaking, and the younger one translated once again.

"These men and the dead who serve them are warriors," they said. "Vakovia is done with war. We are done with war."

Shane waited for a further explanation but received none. If he had more time, he would have pressed for clarity, but he had already wasted too much time standing in the fading light of a burning helicopter.

"We do not want these men in Vakovia."

Shane nodded but said nothing.

"Then it is agreed. We will guide you north and aid you with your enemies as you aid us with ours."

The translator extended his hand, and Shane raised an eyebrow and then took it. The ghost's hand was cold like ice water. They shook, and the other assorted spirits began to drift away.

The old man spoke again, and the translator listened and mulled over the message for a beat before speaking.

"He says that you will probably die. The last one like you died. So, in case you suffer the same fate, he will thank you now for your effort."

"The last one like me died trying to destroy this spirit?" Shane asked. "More than a century ago?"

"Yes," the translator agreed.

The old man wandered off without any more messages, and Shane was left with the translator in the dwindling flames of the King Stallion.

"I will be your first guide," the translator said. "We should go now."

"Yeah," Shane agreed, unsure of what he had just agreed to. Help was help, though. No one would know the Vakovian countryside better than the spirits who haunted it.

"I am Benedikt," the translator said as he led Shane out of the field of grass and away from the flaming debris. He walked into the darkness as though he had followed the same path a thousand times, and Shane went with him.

"Shane," he replied.

"We know your name, Mr. Ryan," the ghost said. "Also, you are American. You are a Marine."

"Retired, and please call me Shane," Shane corrected. "Never came here to fight."

"How quickly our intentions fail us," Benedikt said.

The ghost kept a quick but reasonable pace. Shane's body ached, but he did not slow or complain. They needed distance, and Benedikt was set on it. Their time together was short, however, as Benedikt reached the edge of his range, tethered as he was to his haunted item.

A second ghost waited a short distance away, standing beneath a tall, lonesome oak tree at the edge of another barley field.

"The guides will continue as far as you need to go," Benedikt said.

"They already know?" Shane asked. The ghost nodded.

"This was planned from the time you were in Kogar. But it is good you have agreed to help. If you need anything, ask your guide. Most speak your language, or Russian, or Hungarian, all of which we have heard you speak."

Shane grunted and Benedikt left without saying more.

The next guide was a dour woman with her hair tied under a scarf and a half-burned apron covering her midsection. Her body was charred, but her face was unscathed.

"Alzbeta," the ghost said by way of introduction. She led Shane through a mile of identical field and passed him off to a man named Dudek. Cermak was next, then Lev, Irina, Kristof, Ragnar, Magdalene, Petrov, and Hamish, a Scotsman who had died in Vakovia during the First World War.

Shane traveled the entire night, passed from guide to guide, until dawn encroached on the horizon, bringing a dim, gray light to the sky. With the sun came the sound of another helicopter. His guide, a young woman named Nina, led him to the hollow inside the trunk of a massive sycamore maple. The thick branches and broad leaves provided ample cover, and both stayed out of sight as the helicopter approached and then vanished to the west.

After traveling all night, Shane welcomed the rest. It was better to travel in the dark and remain hidden from the Reapers. He had traveled probably close to thirty miles since Zevna, and he did not think his legs would allow him to keep going.

The hollow in the tree was piled with dried leaves that created a cushioned surface. He leaned into it while the ghost stood next to him, not feeling the same exhaustion he felt but willing to wait for him.

"They say you will kill the demon in the north," Nina said in Polish.

"The demon, huh?" Shane asked.

Nina was younger than most of his guides, probably eighteen at most, and she was as thin as a rail. Her blonde hair was ragged and frizzy, and her skin looked sickly. Only her brown eyes were clear and healthy looking.

"They say it eats other spirits whole."

"Hmm," Shane intoned, unsure what she expected him to say.

"I hear a man like you was sent to fight it once, and the demon pulled the ribs from his body and wore them as a crown."

He had to laugh at that, and the ghost looked offended.

"This is not a joke," she said.

"No, I suppose a rib cage crown wouldn't be funny. Not in person."

"The demon has killed many living and dead. It reigns over a kingdom of bones."

"Sounds like a real jerk," Shane replied. He closed his eyes while Nina continued describing the horror he was headed to.

When Shane opened his eyes again, the sun was high in the sky, and the temperature had increased, though it was still comfortable inside the tree hollow. Nina sat cross-legged at his feet, watching him.

"How long was I asleep?"

"I don't have a watch," she replied unenthusiastically. "It is past midday, though."

Shane squinted at the sky through the trees. It was maybe two or three o'clock by the position of the sun. He'd been asleep at least eight hours.

"Your clothes are full of insects," the ghost pointed out.

He could feel things moving on his skin, the price of sleeping in a pile of dead leaves.

Shane stripped down and shook out his clothes while Nina looked away, struck by a curious case of modesty for a dead person. When he was finished, she pointed to a small pile of fruits and nuts.

"I found these. There is not much to eat," she said.

She had gathered wild raspberries and walnuts as well as two plums.

"Thank you," he said. The food was unexpected but appreciated. He would have preferred a pack of Lucky Strikes, but the food would probably benefit him more in the long run.

He used a rock to smash open the walnuts and ate the fruit quickly before it had a chance to dehydrate in the sun. Nina could find no water within range, but she assured him his next guide could at least take him to a river if he was willing to try drinking from it.

"Did you hear anything while I was asleep?"

"Another helicopter?" she asked. "No. And no other sounds, either. This place is very remote. There is no town for many miles. The nearest road is at least five miles."

"How did you end up out here in the middle of nowhere?"

"It was not always nowhere," she answered, nodding to the fruit. "Those plums came from a tree planted by my grandfather. There was a village once, back the way we came. Not so big. My grandfather fled from Poland during the war and settled here. He planted fruits and vegetables. His brother raised goats. His brother-in-law grew barley. There were others, too. It only took one bomb to destroy it all."

"I'm sorry," Shane said, trying the plum. It was tart but very juicy. He enjoyed it.

"This land has died again and again. But you see, it keeps coming back. The grass, the trees. Me. Everything comes back. Nothing wants to stay dead here."

"Death does seem less... strict in Vakovia," Shane said. The girl smiled.

"It is very strict, but only at first."

"Only at first," Shane repeated.

He finished the fruit and nuts and got to his feet. Waiting until full dark again would be impractical. He was rested and as energized as he could be. If they were so far removed from anything, then it would be safe enough to keep moving. The Reapers with their helicopters gave away their position long before they showed up, so he'd have time to hide if needed.

"Ready to go?" he asked the ghost.

"Yes," she said, leading them back into the open country.

The rest of their mile passed quickly, and soon, Nina passed Shane off to another guide, a middle-aged man with an abundance of warts who went by Shem.

"Take care of yourself, Nina," Shane said as they parted company.

"Stay alive," the girl told him in return.

Shem was not a talker and had nothing to offer Shane on their journey. He did take Shane to the river, however, which was very small compared to the last one Shane had experienced.

The water moved slowly and was murky. Shane had little interest in trying to drink it and risk getting parasites or some sort of industrial pollution poisoning.

Shem waited in sour silence while Shane dug a seep well a couple of yards from the river using rocks and sticks to get down to the water table. He used his T-shirt to line the well as a basic filter and sat there to wait for water to fill the hole.

"You volunteered for this job?" Shane asked the ghost. Shem grunted and Shane nodded. "That's good. Giving back to the community. Noble."

The water slowly filled the hole. He had no container to fill, so he would not be able to carry any with him. Instead, he could only wait until the hole was full enough to use his hand and cup some, drink, and then wait for more. The process was long and dragged them into the late afternoon.

When Shane felt he was hydrated enough and had endured Shem long enough, the two headed off again. Shem did not say goodbye when he handed Shane to his next guide, a boy named Josef.

"Don't suppose you know where any cigarettes are?" he asked. The boy, perhaps ten when he'd died, did not. But he was a better conversationalist than Shem.

Day passed into night and into day again. Ghost guides came and went. Some were friendly, some reserved, and some borderline hostile. Onward they walked. He didn't see a town for an entire week.

"What do you know of the nearest town?" Shane asked his guide, a middle-aged woman named Luda who died of starvation.

"I lived there once," Luda said. "Oba is its name. Terrible place."

Chapter 8
Reapers Calling

Oba was a tiny village of less than two hundred citizens. Luda assured Shane that, while he could probably find some supplies there, it was still a miserable place. Her husband, he had learned, had left her for another woman there.

Luda's feelings aside, Shane was relieved to find civilization. He needed gear if he planned to walk a few hundred more miles across the country. It would take weeks to reach his destination and destroy the ghost most of them referred to as a demon.

All Shane had with him were boots and a lighter that didn't work. He needed a water bottle, a knife, and other tools for survival in the wild, even only the most basic ones. Having ghosts gather food and point out water was helpful, but it was the bare minimum. He needed to do better. Especially if he was going to face off against some legendary monster. He wouldn't have the strength on a diet of nuts and berries.

It was early evening as they approached the village, and few people were out and about. Lights could be seen through windows and smoke rose from chimneys. Some of the houses smelled of roasting meat, and the scent of coffee carried over from somewhere. Shane had not realized how much he missed coffee until that time.

He had told Luda what he wanted to find, and she had gone off in search of easy targets. She'd found a reasonable knife for him in the back of an old pickup truck within minutes.

He found the backpack on his own, hanging next to laundry on a clothesline in someone's backyard. It was not military, but it had straps, and it closed with a drawstring, and that was enough. He stole a sweater as well and slinked away quickly before the owners saw anything.

Luda found some rope and a small hatchet, both of which Shane slipped into his backpack. A water bottle was harder to find, but she located one inside another house.

"The owners are upstairs; they'll never notice," she assured him. "They have a better knife, too. And better bags. You can get everything you need in this one house."

Shane followed the ghost through trees and fields behind houses until she brought him to the one she'd found. It was a small building, a little more ramshackle than some of the others, with a thick plume of smoke coming from the chimney and no lights in any of the windows.

"Why is it dark?" Shane asked, crouching behind the house to observe.

"How would I know?" the old woman replied.

"What are the people inside doing?"

"Just sitting around. I did not get a good look. Oba is not an exciting village. People do not do much here."

"Do you know them?"

She looked at him like he was foolish.

"Why would I know these people?"

"You said you used to live here."

"Fifty years ago," she pointed out. "I do not come here now unless I need to."

Shane grunted and got to his feet, running while hunched low toward the back door of the home. Luda came with him and entered the house before returning quickly.

"It is clear," she said.

Shane opened the rear door of the house slowly and silently. The door led to the kitchen and an adjoining dining area. Luda pointed to the dining table and Shane froze.

Three black packs had been dumped on the table, each bulging with gear.

"This is a good knife," the ghost said, pointing to the tactical knife with a compass in the hilt sticking out of one. "And water bottle."

Shane waved a hand to silence her. The packs were identical to the ones he'd seen carried by Reaper Company mercenaries so far.

Footsteps thumped across the floor upstairs, and Shane grimaced. The soldiers were up there, probably observing through windows. Their spectral assets were another matter. Luda had mentioned nothing about ghosts.

Shane grabbed one of the packs off of the table and hurried back toward the door, waving for his guide to come with him. She did as bidden, confused by his actions, and they hit the yard.

"You are acting—" Luda began.

"Shh," Shane hushed, waving her to the side of the house. He glanced up and noticed there was no window at the rear of the home, but there were side windows and likely a front one. The house was in the middle of the street, inconspicuous to any normal observer. Shane never would have looked twice at it if Luda hadn't scouted it. It was a discreet base for the Reapers if they were observing the village to see who passed through.

There was a truck parked next to the house. Not a black SUV like the Reapers usually drove, but a newer-model pickup truck. Shane pulled the knife from the pack and stabbed two of the tires.

"These are the people I'm running from," Shane told Luda, crouching between the crippled truck and the house. The ghost's eyes widened.

"I thought it was men in a helicopter," she said. The whisper network, it seemed, was not without its weaknesses.

"They got out of the helicopter," he told her.

Shane dug through the pack he'd stolen. He tossed out a GPS unit and the radio in case it could be tracked as well. There were a number of clips for a rifle and rounds for a pistol that was also missing alongside items of more immediate use like rations, matches, and even a folding shovel. In the front pocket, in a secure case, was a single claymore.

His gut told him to leave before anyone found the pack missing. But he knew they'd come looking. He needed the supplies, and he had the upper hand. It was only going to last minutes at most.

"Watch my back," Shane said.

They circled the house to the door again. Shane opened it and headed into the kitchen. He wedged a stick from the yard under the door to keep it open and took out the claymore, setting it up on its tiny, metal feet right in the doorway. There were murmurs of conversation from the second floor and more heavy footsteps. He worked quickly, attaching the blasting cap that came with the claymore into the adapter and jamming it into the mine.

He unspooled the wire connected to the cap and tied it around the stick wedged in the door, then unrolled it as far as it would go back into the yard, giving him about one spare yard as he ducked behind a tree.

"Is that a bomb?" Luda asked.

"Something like that. I need you to go back to the door and just yell."

"Yell what?" she asked.

"Yell anything," Shane told her as he rigged the firing mechanism to the wire. "Be quick."

The ghost did as she was instructed. Shane unlocked the firing mechanism and waited. The ghost reached the door and screamed.

The sound was piercing and inhuman. Shane's skin prickled with goosebumps, but it worked. A spirit dropped through the floor as three Reapers came down the stairs. Shane waited until they were together on the main floor and squeezed the handle.

The C4 in the mine exploded. Hundreds of steel balls erupted and tore through the house as smoke filled the air. Glass and wood shattered, and the house rumbled, shifting on its foundation.

He had forgotten about the other two packs on the table. Both claymores were set off by the blast, and the explosion collapsed the front half of the house. Shrapnel flew in all directions and the earth underfoot shook as the house fell in on itself.

Shane ran into the fray, not waiting for the smoke to clear. He found the ghost that had come down first, stunned by the attack and standing dumbstruck right where it had first appeared in the rubble of the building.

He sprinted through the smoke and elbowed the ghost in the jaw. The ghost's head snapped right as bone broke, and Shane dragged him to the ground. He snapped the ghost's neck and twisted the head a full one-eighty before pulling.

The blast of energy from the ghost further destabilized the ruins of the house and the final remnants of the frame collapsed. Shane stumbled through what remained, back to the yard, and snatched up the stolen pack.

"That was remarkable," Luda said.

"Two ghosts are missing. We need to go before they get back," he told her.

"You must mean them," Luda replied.

Two spirits drifted through the rubble of the house, one at either side of the ruins so that they were primed to flank Shane as they approached him. The ghost on the left was a tall, thin spirit whose flesh was peeling away from the muscle across his face, and the other was shorter, with broken ribs piercing his clothing.

Shane backed away slowly, watching both spirits as the street behind them filled with Oba's residents, both living and dead, drawn out by the explosion to see what had happened.

"This has been exciting," Luda told Shane. She smiled at him and nodded. "Put on that pack and keep heading north."

She left him without waiting for his reply. The spectral assets saw the woman's ghost approaching them but paid her no mind. To her credit, she ignored them at first.

Luda passed through the destroyed house to the street beyond, her form fading in and out of view in the smoke. Shane continued backing into the field behind the house.

"You can't run fast enough," the broken-ribbed ghost told him in a faintly southern accent. The spirit's lip had curled into a sneer. Peeled Face, whose flesh was pulling his lips in several directions from his mouth, said nothing.

"I'll give you guys credit," Shane said. "No matter how many of you I destroy, you're always confident you'll be the one who somehow survives."

Ribs looked at the other ghost as though maybe Shane's words resonated for just a moment, but it was fleeting. Neither stopped.

While Shane backed off, more spirits came through the ruins. Neither of the spectral assets turned to see them, but Shane saw them clearly. First a farmer, thin and desiccated, his flesh stained yellow and his eyes sunken. Then a burlier man, his hands black with grease and a bloody wound caving in half of his skull. More followed them.

A woman with a deep bruise circling her neck was followed by two young men whose bodies were bent and broken. Luda was with them, and another old man who was as white as a sheet.

"You don't belong here," Luda called out.

The two ghosts were caught by surprise and turned to see what was behind them. A dozen ghosts had gathered and were filtering through the rubble of the house, circling the spectral assets.

"Who the hell are you?" Ribs asked.

"Vakovia's dead," Luda replied.

"Well, la-di-da," Ribs mocked. "Go back to your goddamn holes in the ground, then."

The ghost with greasy hands grabbed the spirit with the peeling flesh and took hold of one of the curls of dry skin hanging from his face. He pulled and tore the asset's face in half, stripping the flesh like it was carpet from the ghost's mouth to his hairline.

The farmer held the ghost down as it struggled, and more joined in. They tore pieces off the ghost and threw them into the building's rubble.

Stray bits of flesh gave way to more permanent features. Ears were pulled away, and then they worked lower on the body. Ribs aided his partner, but Luda and the others converged. It was like a flock of vultures on carrion, pulling away chunk after chunk.

The spectral assets fought back, but they were overwhelmed by the numbers. Fingers and then hands and arms were broken and torn and discarded.

Shane did not wait to watch the scene play out. He knew how it would end, and he had no time to spare. He shouldered his pack and ran, traveling around Oba as quickly as he could to get back on the path north.

The Reapers would have had no time to call in for help. The others would only know they were missing when radio contact couldn't be established. It could be fifteen minutes or six hours. Shane would be long gone.

Oba was gone from sight when he saw a ghost in the near distance, waiting in the open countryside for him. It was a child this time, a girl not much older than Eloise, with raven-black hair and a dress stained with old, dried blood.

"I will guide you north," the girl said, approaching him. Shane looked back the way he had come and saw nothing but darkness.

"You're the next guide, huh? Lost sight of my last one in a village," he told her.

"I know," she said. The whisper network spread word quickly. "Come. It gets harder to travel in some places. You should move fast."

Chapter 9
The Noose Grows Tight

Reaper air patrols were more present than ever. They had commandeered a Vakovian chopper, smaller than the King Stallions but still capable of recon from the air, and were flying routine runs. The frequency of their passes was no coincidence. They were covering the northern paths away from Oba.

Shane had drawn them a straight line from Zevna to Oba. The Reapers knew where he'd been and were easily able to make guesses about where he was going. He had scouted a small town two days from Oba and found it crawling with Reapers and their assets, despite them trying to stay out of sight.

His one advantage was that they did not know Vakovia's dead were helping him, but that would not last long either if he kept handing the Reapers information about his location. He needed to change plans.

Pavel was the name of Shane's most recent guide. He was a shaky young man in dirty coveralls who was missing half an arm.

"What's east of here?" Shane asked him midway through their journey. They were traveling at night and sticking to forested area to avoid being spotted in the sky. Reapers made passes almost hourly, using a search grid with two helicopters to locate him.

"Not much. Ulenka, I think. But it is far from here. Maybe Taska to the northeast," Pavel replied.

"And Slovakia?"

"Yes," Pavel agreed. "But it is many days' journey."

Shane nodded, fixing his sights to the east.

"Ulenka. That's a town?"

"A small village. It used to be larger, but much was abandoned. I think people still live there."

"Let's go to Ulenka," Shane suggested.

"We're supposed to keep going north," Pavel said.

"I know. That's why we should go east."

Pavel's expression was a mask of confusion.

"But we go north."

"They go north," Shane said, pointing to the sky. "They're waiting for me. If we keep going north, they're going to be where I need to go before I get there. We need to give them a new trail to follow."

"But—"

"I'll be dead before I get wherever you want me to go, and your demon will keep being demonic and nothing will change. Trust me," Shane said. Pavel looked sullen.

"They will be upset," the ghost said.

"Who will be?"

"The others," he said vaguely.

"I will be more upset if you guide me into an ambush and my head gets blown off."

The ghost had little to say to counter that, and Shane nodded to the east.

"Let's go find Ulenka."

Pavel did as requested, taking Shane east instead of north. They were cutting back toward what he avoided for some time, back in the general direction of Ravjek, though he was much farther north now, and the Slovakia border.

With a little prompting and a few breadcrumbs, he was sure he could get the Reapers on a new trail. He didn't want it to be too obvious, though. No setting fires to cook his dinner, but if he ducked into a little town and destroyed another two or three spectral assets, and took out another one of the Reaper's vehicles, that ought to be enough to set them off in a new direction.

Pavel passed Shane to another ghost, equally unhappy to be traveling east, and then several more who mostly felt the same way. They had been told the plan was north, and they all wanted to go north. Each time Shane had to explain the problem. The days grew hotter once again, and his patience wore thin with trying to explain himself.

He had tried to convince the spirits to at least spy for him. Their ability to get messages ahead of themselves through a chain of the dead was impressive. He did something, and ghosts for miles ahead knew he had done it. But if he needed them to scout towns and search for the Reapers, they were less inclined to be of service.

"How can I scout a town if I am here with you?" a ghost named Uli asked.

"You tell the other ghosts and spread it down the line, then have some go and check."

"But we are supposed to go north, not spy on towns," the ghost insisted. In some ways, it was like talking to the trees.

After a day of traveling east, they were in sight of the town of Ulenka. As Pavel had assured him the day before, it was not a place that was in good condition. Many homes had collapsed and stood as little more than piles of rotten wood in overgrown fields. But there were a few buildings still standing that would serve their purpose.

There were no Reapers in the town yet, but their scouting patterns had gone far enough to have seen the town from the sky. Shane had not shown up in any of the northern points they would have been watching after Oba, and soon enough, they would have to assume he went a different direction. Ulenka was an obvious target.

Shane and his guide, a middle-aged woman named Ella, approached the town slowly. He stayed low in the trees beyond one of the overgrown fields while the ghost ventured into the town to check things out. She returned within fifteen minutes.

"None of your Reapers," she told him. "Only a few townspeople, maybe three dozen. Two homes have dead you should avoid. They lurk in shadow and will not tolerate the living."

Shane grunted. It was a solid recon report. He could have used Ella for the long haul, but he knew that was not the deal. None of the spirits wanted to leave their homes to go with him. They traveled their mile and nothing more.

"What about that?" he asked, pointing out the barn at the eastern edge of the village.

"Empty," the ghost replied. "Nothing of value inside that I could see. Just hay and rusty tools."

"Sounds perfect," Shane said.

He made his way up the property, keeping low enough to avoid detection by the scant few residents of the village and the unsavory dead who disliked interacting with the living.

Ella followed him into the barn and watched him scout the area. It had not been used in years from the state of it, but the structure was still sound. The weathered wood was plain and unpainted, but it had held up to the weather with minimal warping. Outside, they were sun-bleached to a nearly bone white, but inside, they were silvery gray. The building was unusually long compared to its width.

The double doors to the barn opened on screeching hinges. Ella winced at the sound, but Shane grinned. He pulled the door open and shut a couple of times, listening to the groan of the rusty metal. It was perfect.

"Can you cover this?" he asked, indicating his footprints in the dust on the floorboards. The ghost looked at it and swished her foot lightly. His footprints vanished as dust settled over them again, as though he had never been there. He smiled and nodded.

"This will work," he said, more to himself than her.

Shane set about rearranging the barn, stacking hay from the center against the wall near the door and then all along the exterior wall to the rear of the building. Ella moved along after him, forcing the smallest bits into the piles and rearranging the dust so it looked like the barn had been as it had been for ages.

Crates and boxes were stacked near the entrance. Once the hay was in place, Shane began filling the opposite side of the barn with the boxes, making a clear division that was separated by a waist-high center wall. To the right was an open path bordered by hay. From the door, it gave a clear view right to the back wall and was relatively clean and open. Anyone entering the barn would glance once and ignore it.

To the left, he lined the walls with fallen tools. Rusty scythes, hammers, saws, chains, whatever he found scattered around the floor. For the floor, he made a maze of crates and containers. A hundred places to hide and enough clutter to ensure anyone really searching would have to journey all the way to the back wall and search every corner.

The setup took hours. The sun would rise soon. Shane returned to the front of the barn to look over his handiwork. He drank water from the bottle and ate some fruit and vegetables Ella had helped him harvest.

"What now?" she asked.

"We wait," Shane answered.

Nothing happened on the first day. He waited in the dark, as he had staked out the barn at the orchard what seemed like forever ago. He saw one villager leave town and return six hours later. A helicopter flew over the town to the north and then doubled back after a short while. He watched between cracks in the barnboards as it circled the village and then left.

"That's it," he said.

Ella looked out at the sky as the helicopter left.

"They are leaving."

"They'll be back. On the ground next time. Tomorrow," he said. It would be risky to show up at night, given their track record. They would wait until first light and then roll in. If they had checked a handful of other towns already, they'd be sloppy, too. Reaper Company was not as elite as it thought it was.

"You sound certain," the ghost told him.

"Pretty certain. Their commanding officer is predictable. Not a lot of experience commanding in the field, I bet. Probably took most of his orders from the Colonel."

"Who is the Colonel?" Ella asked.

"A dead man."

"You killed him?"

"We had a disagreement over who wanted to live more."

"Why do these men all want you dead?"

"Because they killed someone I used to know, and I didn't like it."

"They want to cover their crime?" Ella asked.

"Many crimes," Shane corrected.

"I hope you kill them all, then," the ghost said.

It had not been his plan to do such a thing, but it was starting to look like it was his only way out. He'd kill every Reaper that came after him if he had to.

Night came, and Shane tweaked his setup one last time. He stacked more hay and left a pitchfork in the front stack, a long-reach weapon he could use in a pinch if need be.

When the sun rose, Shane was already awake. He had left briefly in the night, found water, and made mud. His body was covered in it, a quick camouflage for the dirty barn.

As the sun rose higher, the barn grew hot. Ella asked when the men would come, and Shane said nothing. Three hours passed before she got her answer.

The roar of an engine broke the stillness of Ulenka. A trail of dust in the distance gave away their position as a vehicle wound down the dry, dusty road into the village. Shane retreated from the door as a black SUV came to a stop right at the outskirts of town. He watched between slats as a man and a ghost exited the vehicle. Just the pair of them. They didn't think Ulenka was a serious target, then.

The ghost left his partner and headed for the barn. It was the first structure in the village, the most obvious of all targets. It was as Shane had intended.

He pulled away from the door and crawled into the hay. Ella crouched in the pile with him, hidden from view.

The spirit entered the barn and stood still, looking at everything. A long moment passed, and then the hinges screamed as the door was pulled open. Amid the piles of hay, Shane could just make out the shapes and positions of the ghost and now the man in the doorway.

"Anything?" the soldier asked.

"Not yet," the ghost replied. He floated to the more cluttered side of the barn, the place where someone was more likely to be hidden, and started to search.

Shane had taken advantage of the barn's unusual length. The path to the rear was enticing and obscured. There were many places to hide, and a lot of clutter that blocked the view of the rear which would, in turn, block the view of the entrance once someone was far enough back.

Reapers used ghosts as scouts. It was a smart thing to do. It was also dangerous. Letting the one who couldn't die go first only worked if what they were looking for was ahead of them. The soldier stayed alone at the entrance.

Shane watched the man pace, a rifle held firmly in his grip.

"When I go, get the gun. No sound," Shane mouthed to Ella. The ghost nodded.

The spectral asset had ventured past where it could be seen. The soldier turned his back on the hay pile and began pacing toward the door. Shane and Ella rose from the pile without a sound.

Ella swooped low toward the Reaper as Shane raised the pitchfork. It was three paces to the man in the doorway. He strode with purpose, speed, and force. The tines of the fork sunk into the back of the man's head.

The ghost eased him to the ground as he fell, laying him out as though putting him down for a nap. Shane looked back to the rear of the barn and could see nothing. He leaned down quickly, dousing two fingers in the puddle of blood on the floor and then scrawling hasty letters across the barn door.

"What are you doing?" Ella whispered.

"You'll see," he mouthed back, cleaning his hands in the dust and then gesturing for her to follow him back to their hiding place.

"Clear," the ghost yelled from the rear of the barn. Ella pulled the hay back into place around them, leaving the pile pristine and undisturbed.

With no answer from his partner, the ghost rushed to the front of the barn. He found his partner face-down on the ground and then looked around quickly, scanning for signs of the enemy. He saw nothing.

The spirit turned the dead man over, looking down into his face. The pitchfork clattered, and the hinges on the door whined as it began to swing. It closed with a thump and the ghost looked up, seeing the words written in blood for the first time.

BEHIND YOU

Chapter 10
All Roads

The ghost turned quickly, but there was nothing there. Shane and Ella remained hidden.

"You're going to die!" the ghost yelled at nothing. He turned his back, looking at the door once more, and Shane rose to his feet. The soft rustling of hay caught the ghost's ear, and he turned back.

"It's you," the ghost said with a hiss as his eyes fell on Shane.

"It is," Shane agreed.

He ran at the ghost, surprising him with the speed and force of the attack. Shane's strikes hit hard and revealed the ghost's lack of preparedness. He threw the ghost to the ground.

"How?" the spirit gasped. Surely, they had all heard Shane could fight them by now, even destroy them, and still, they didn't want to believe it.

Shane had no time for explanations. His hand clashed with the ghost's mouth, breaking his jaw. The ghost writhed and squirmed like something inhuman, and Shane pushed harder. Both hands compressed the spectral asset's skull, and moments later, it crunched and then collapsed.

The spirit burst, and the barn rumbled. Dust exploded in all directions as though a bomb had gone off, and Shane coughed as he was thrown against the door.

The hinges shrieked, and the door flew open under Shane's weight. He landed hard on the ground outside, under plumes of slow-moving dust that billowed from the doorway.

Ella came out a moment later and stood over him, looking down at him with an expression that was hard to identify.

"Is that how all the dead die?" she asked.

"More or less," Shane replied. "It's volatile."

"It felt… powerful," she said, savoring the word.

"I've heard it can be a bit of a rush," he replied. The violent explosion of spirit energy could be absorbed, at least in part, by other ghosts. Some ghosts fed on others and grew stronger. Maybe that was the nature of the demon in the north they were all so afraid of.

"I see now why they want you in the north. I have never seen anything like that," Ella told him.

"Happy to do it, if I can get there in one piece."

"You might need more help than we thought at first. I have an idea," the ghost suggested.

"A car would be great. Maybe a Blackhawk."

"I will be back," she said, drifting off before he could ask where or how long she might be.

Shane searched through the Reaper's belongings, hoping for a pack of cigarettes. The big man had nothing on him, and Shane cursed. Killers for hire, and not a single one of them smoked that he'd found so far. It was maddening.

The SUV still waited on the road where the man had parked it. It was possible he'd left something inside, or at least some more gear Shane could make use of. He was not sure where Ella had gone, but she would catch up soon enough.

Time was ticking for Ulenka. The SUV was probably being tracked, and the dead man would be expected to radio in soon. Shane had a small window to search the vehicle before he needed to flee again. But the Reapers would know he had turned east, and they would be forced to keep searching in that direction. Even if they thought it was a misdirection, they couldn't afford to ignore it. At best, their forces would be cut in half covering the north and the east.

The SUV had no cigarettes inside. He found some bottled water, more

MREs, and a bag of Russian potato chips. There was little else of value.

He pulled out the bag of chips and popped it open. The label said they were crab-flavored, which he wasn't enthused about, but he'd eaten nothing beyond fruit and nuts for days.

"Shouldn't take food without asking," a Texan voice said.

The sound of a gun being cocked preceded it, and Shane felt the barrel press to the back of his head. He glanced at the window of the SUV and saw the reflection of two men behind him.

Another soldier came from the left and one more circled the SUV to his right. He could only see two of the spectral assets directly but assumed the other two were behind him as well.

They had sent five men into Ulenka; one had just showed up alone in his own SUV. Shane should have guessed he wasn't so lucky.

"I'm willing to share," he said, holding up the bag of chips. The second man behind him swatted the bag from his hands.

"Nice and slow, Ryan. Hands behind your back," the Texan said.

He had four guns on him. If there was a clever way out of the situation, Shane wasn't sure what it was. If he fought, he'd be dead before he turned around.

"Maybe we can talk about a deal. I saw some change in the center console—" Shane began. One of the men slammed his head against the door of the SUV, and a second gun, this one a pistol, was forced against his temple.

"Those guys you killed outside of Zevna were my squad," the second man said. His voice was deeper than the first man's, but in a way that sounded almost forced like he was trying to sound tough. Shane chuckled, and his head was slammed against the door again.

"You think this is funny?" he growled, twisting the gun harder into Shane's temple.

"No," Shane said, unable to get a good look at his assailant from the angle. "You just sound like you're dying to go to the bathroom or something."

One of the other Reapers barked a laugh, and the man with his gun on Shane shifted.

"You want to be next, Bloom?"

"That's enough," the Texan interrupted. "Just cuff him."

"I'm gonna be there when you die," the tough guy said, his lips nearly on Shane's ear as he pressed him hard to the door. "I'm gonna watch you bleed."

"I'm gonna watch you bleed," Shane repeated, forcing his voice dramatically deeper. The other man, Bloom, laughed again.

Shane's wrists were pulled back sharply, and he felt something slip around them. A loud zipping sound preceded the feeling of the band tightening and his wrists being forced together.

The man restraining him pulled him off the SUV and turned him around, slamming him against the door again. Shane could see everyone now, four men and four ghosts.

Tough Guy was about what Shane had expected. Thin and wiry, with a craggy, gaunt face and three days of stubble. The taller man behind him, the Texan, looked like a Varsity running back. Broad shoulders, shaved head, a square jaw, and keen eyes. No one wore a rank insignia, but he was clearly in command.

On either side were a pair of younger soldiers, barely in their twenties. Bloom, on Shane's right, was gawky and thin, but the other one must have spent an inordinate amount of time working out.

Their spectral assets were a mishmash of a freakshow. One burn victim, two bloody messes, and a fourth, attached to the Texan, looked like an accountant with no visible signs of trauma. The ghost could have stood in any elevator in Boston, and no one would have batted an eye.

"Brightburn, this is Wolf Six, come in," the Texan said into his radio.

"Wolf Six?" Shane said. "Very Schwarzenegger. You guys are cool."

Tough Guy pressed his gun to Shane's forehead again and leaned in close.

"You must not want to live long," he said, teeth clenched. Shane smiled.

"You got me, big guy. I'm not long for this world. Pull the trigger."

Tough Guy grimaced and pressed the gun harder against Shane, forcing his head against the SUV window.

"I'll do it," he hissed.

"I'm sure you will. Should I set an egg timer, or…?"

Tough Guy cursed and punched him in the gut. Shane laughed as he doubled over, taking a moment to catch his breath before righting himself.

"That wasn't your gun. Does he get left and right confused a lot?" he asked the other Reapers. Bloom laughed again and Tough Guy raised his weapon, smashing it against the side of Shane's face. He felt a tooth come loose and spit out a mouthful of blood before smiling again.

"Strike two," Shane said. Tough Guy raised his gun once more.

"Stand down, Owen," the Texan ordered.

"The hell do you mean 'stand down'?" he asked.

"You forget basic orders?" Texan asked.

"Wolf Six this is Brightburn, report," a voice over the radio crackled.

The Texan kept his eyes on Tough Guy Owen and raised the radio.

"We've got target in custody, need confirmation on rendezvous," Texan said.

"Proceed to Ravjek," the radio voice responded.

"Ravjek confirmed. Over," Texan said, putting the radio back in a holster on his hip.

Shane saw Ella in the woods beyond the men and their ghosts. Her eyes locked on his, and he shook his head very slightly. She retreated back into the trees.

"Put him in the back. Bloom and Levy, take the other truck and follow."

"On it," Bloom said, leaving with the fourth man. Tough Guy Owen pushed Shane toward the rear of the SUV and opened the back. Once he was out of sight of the Texan, he punched Shane in the gut again.

"The only reason you're still alive is because the Major wants you that way."

"Is the only reason you're still alive because no one wanted to waste a bullet?" Shane asked.

Owen punched him in the gut again and then pushed him into the back of the SUV, face-down on the mat, and closed the door. The two men talked outside for a few minutes before they both got in with their spectral assets and the engine rumbled to life.

The SUV turned around, and then they were underway. Shane could just barely see the rear windshield, and even then, all he could see were dust clouds forming behind them.

They had traveled for all of thirty seconds when something plowed into the SUV. Shane was slammed against the rear door and then back to the rear seat as the vehicle spun and then flipped. It rolled over, and Shane was dumped to the ceiling, the windows, the floor, and back again, over and over. The sound of shattering glass and crunching metal filled the void.

Shane was upside-down when the vehicle came to a rest next to a tree. He was covered in small cuts but otherwise unscathed. The rear windshield had been smashed. Hands still bound, he crawled from the opening into a field of grass alongside the road.

"I hear you need help."

On his knees, hands bound behind his back, Shane looked up. A ghost loomed over him like nothing he had ever seen. It was a man, or arguably a man, as big as any living thing Shane had ever seen. He was more like a bear, shirtless to the waist, and covered in thick, black hair across his chest and shoulders and arms.

"Huh," Shane said. The ghost leaned down and pulled the zip tie from Shane's wrist, snapping it like an elastic.

"Oleg the Brute is here. Oleg never loses."

The big ghost laughed and beat his chest with a fist the size of a ham. He reminded Shane of Andre the Giant, only more feral.

The spectral assets were first to extricate themselves from the SUV, which was now upside down in a ravine. Oleg, whoever he was, had flipped the vehicle over by knocking it right off the road and into a tree.

The colossal spirit was on top of the Texan's accountant spirit like a cat on a mouse. He wrenched the ghost's head off his body in seconds, absorbing the blast like it was nothing and moving onto Owen's burned companion.

The new ghost was better prepared, and at least sparred with Oleg for a moment before the larger ghost crushed his head.

Gunshots from the road forced Shane to scramble behind the SUV. The other Reapers in the second vehicle were firing on them.

"Oleg the Brute never loses," the massive ghost yelled at them. He ran from the ravine.

Shane moved to the front of the SUV where the others couldn't see him. He crouched next to the windshield for a heartbeat before Tough Guy Owen raised an arm and pointed his gun at Shane from the seat where he was still belted.

Owen's face was a mask of blood. Glass was embedded in his flesh, and one eye was swollen shut.

"Told you I was gonna watch you die," the man said. His arm shook, and he tried to pull the trigger but could not. Shane could see a tear in his sleeve and a large wound along his forearm that bled openly. If the arm wasn't fractured, the muscle had been damaged. He didn't have the strength to pull a trigger.

"I bet you say a lot of things that aren't true," Shane replied. He reached in and pulled the gun from his hand.

The Texan was trying to pull his radio from his side to call for help, but his hands were too shaky to get any grip. Shane pulled it away from him and tossed it into the grass.

"You guys want me to shoot you or leave you here to see what happens?" Shane asked.

He could see a steady drip of blood running down the side of the Texan's face. A branch from the tree they'd struck had pierced the side of his neck. It was only the size of a finger, but it was more than enough. He'd be dead in minutes.

"You leave me here, and I'll hunt you down," Owen said. "I'll track you across the goddamn world if I have to."

"No, you won't," Shane said.

He could see another wound in Owen's gut. Blood was running in a steady stream. Neither man would survive the hour. He left them there while Owen screamed after him, eventually choking and falling silent.

On the road, Oleg had finished with both the ghosts and the men.

"Two soldiers and four ghosts in what, five minutes?" Shane said.

"Champion of the Iron Tournament," Oleg said, slamming his chest again.

"That a fact?" Shane replied.

"No one kills like Oleg."

Chapter 11
Civilization

Oleg the Brute had been in the Iron Tournament for decades in Europe, mostly Russia, an offshoot of the same Boston tournament Shane had once been forced to join by an ancient ghost called Lazarus. He was supposed to have been returned to a place in Vakovia, which was a different country when he was born, but his wish was never fulfilled. The person carrying his haunted item had died in Ulenka, and so Oleg had haunted the village and surrounding area for many years.

"Here," the burly ghost said as he led Shane back to the village.

In the basement of one of the abandoned homes, in a rusty old box, was a pile of rags. Shane unwrapped them and revealed an antique dagger made of gold. It was purely ornamental and adorned with several pearls and gemstones. The craftsmanship was amazing. It had to be worth tens of thousands of dollars.

"This is the item you're attached to?" Shane asked.

"Yes," Oleg replied. "It is very precious."

"You'll have to tell me the story later," Shane said, wrapping it back in the rags, and slipping it into his pack. He was going to bury it once they reached their destination, where Oleg originally wanted to be buried.

Oleg would come with him for the rest of his journey, it had been decided. Essentially a ghost bodyguard, for when the Reapers came at him in force again.

Shane raided the fallen Reapers, taking more supplies, cash, and food. He left the still-functional SUV, and he and Oleg headed overland after a quick goodbye to Ella, who had tracked down Oleg for him.

They ran north again and kept up the pace for an hour. Oleg, for all his size, felt no exhaustion and no physical limitations, so he could run forever. Shane did his best to keep up.

"The dagger belonged to my grandfather," Oleg explained once they had put more than an hour between themselves and the fallen Reapers.

He felt they would have more of a buffer this time since the Texan had confirmed they were taking Shane to Ravjek. No one would be looking, and no one would expect him for hours. There might be a scheduled check-in, but it would be a long time coming.

"Your grandfather had expensive taste," Shane commented.

"He was a great man! Only the best for Ivar Sigurdsson."

"Sigurdsson," Shane repeated. "You're from Sweden or Iceland or thereabouts?"

Oleg bellowed and scowled at Shane.

"Norge! Not Sweden. That is a name from you Englishmen."

"Norway," Shane stated.

"Norge," the ghost corrected. It was the same place, but clearly, Oleg didn't enjoy the anglicized version. Shane didn't press it.

"Why did you want to be in Vakovia and not Norge?" Shane asked.

"I had a family here," Oleg said proudly. "As a man. A living man like you. This was my home. And in the north, that was where I was meant to be. But the Iron Tournament took me far. Many lands. Many languages. Many deaths. And when they told me I won my freedom, this was where I wanted to be."

"Then we'll make sure we get you home," Shane told him.

Oleg chuckled and looked at him.

"Yes. You must live long enough!"

Oleg knew the land around Vakovia better than most, and he was more willing than Shane's previous guides to deviate from any specific track. He had no interest in getting to the north right away and was happy to go wherever Shane deemed necessary. The ghost had a love for travel that bordered on touristy.

"The Reapers are going to be scouring the countryside. It's where I've been for long enough now that they'll expect I'll stick to the plan. I think we need to find a town," Shane suggested.

"A big town?" Oleg asked.

"Sure," Shane agreed. He could get lost in an urban area easily enough. He knew to avoid the police already, and he could disguise himself if need be. The Reapers would be less inclined to look for him in a large population for just those reasons.

"I know where to go," the ghost said.

They deviated from the path, heading northeast and traveling through some of the most vibrant country Shane had seen so far. Here the land was most alive, with many streams and rivers, and farms full of well-tended crops and livestock.

Shane stole eggs and pilfered produce where he could, using them to supplement his stolen MREs. He was eating better than he had in some time and feeling stronger after his merciless beating in the river and weeks on the run.

Oleg led them on safe paths that never came close to the living, and days had passed without even a sign of a helicopter. Finally, they crested a rise in a plum orchard, and Oleg pointed out what lay below.

"Mostava," the ghost said.

The city was the largest Shane had seen next to Ravjek. It was much larger than Seeburg or even Kogar. The downtown was full of large obelisks and domed towers. Like Ravjek, ancient architecture was mixed with new. Pale, green, copper domes on churches and historic landmarks were nestled among the taller glass edifices that housed offices and high-priced apartments for the few in Vakovia who made money and could afford such luxuries.

"It looks very different than I remember," Oleg said.

"Progress," Shane said, watching cars stream in and out of the city from a distance, and boats come to port along a wide expanse of river. Somewhere in that city was a pack of cigarettes.

"Let's go," Shane said. He led the way down the hillside and toward the first real civilization he'd seen in weeks.

Cars zipped past Shane as he walked down the shoulder of the road to Mostava. Oleg was at his side, unseen to all save the other spirits that roamed the countryside. They passed pedestrians, farmers, and city-dwellers, none of whom could see the beast who traveled at Shane's side.

The city crept up slowly as farmland gave way to smaller houses that were built closer and closer together until they reached a place where two streets intersected. There was a gas station on the corner, and Shane could have kissed the ground in front of it.

"You need to clean up," Oleg advised him. He was still covered in mud from Ulenka. He also smelled like a man who had been walking across a country for weeks and had yet to bathe.

"Yeah," Shane agreed. He went to the bathroom located on the side of the building and headed inside, seeing himself in the mirror for the first time since his hotel in Ravjek.

Aside from the mud, he was covered in scrapes and scabs. He had lost more weight than was healthy, he guessed, and he was starting to look like some of the ghosts he'd seen on his travels. His eyes looked sunken, and his cheeks were recessed. He needed a real meal. And maybe to not walk for forty miles every day.

He washed his face and then stripped down, washing the rest of his body in the small, rusted-out gas station sink. It was not his proudest moment, but he felt better for having done it. When he finished, Oleg was in the parking lot out front.

"This market is full of unusual things," the ghost warned.

Oleg had been in Ulenka for decades. He had missed the rise of junk food, plastic wrappers, blue sports drinks, and everything else a gas station stocked. He was not ready for the modern world.

"Lucky Strikes?" Shane asked the middle-aged man at the gas station counter. The man stared at Shane like he had spoken gibberish. He asked again in another language and got nothing before asking for cigarettes.

He bought two packs of a local brand since they had no American cigarettes, a hat, and picked up a coffee that would probably have been terrible at any other time but, at that moment, was the best cup he'd ever had. The man at the counter gave him directions to a hotel, and he left.

Shane slipped the hat on and headed down the road again with Oleg at his side.

"Just a night," Shane assured Oleg. "Some real sleep in a bed, a hot meal for a change of pace, and we're back on the road tomorrow."

Oleg shrugged. He did not care, and Shane was happy about that. They soon found walking paths, and the city gave way to the ancient one with its fancy bridges and antiquated buildings.

Mostava was full of parks and greenery. Even the modern parts of the town had been built to at least blend in with the older zones. It was not half as dirty as Ravjek, and while it had an abundance of spirits, the living were more abundant as well.

People rode bicycles and scooters. Compact cars wound through mazes of cobblestone streets, and the smells of a hundred meals being cooked were around every corner.

The dead of Mostava stared at Oleg as he passed. Some spoke to him in a variety of languages, most of which he answered in their native tongue. Oleg had traveled far with the Iron Tournament and had learned many languages since his death.

Shane found the hotel that the gas station attendant had recommended. It was small but clean and in a good part of town. It didn't stand out as a place someone on the run might hole up in.

He used the rest of the money he'd stolen from the Reapers to rent a room with a fake name, kept his hat on and his head down most of the time, and spoke Russian to seem as inconspicuous as possible. The clerk at the desk handed him his keys and didn't give him another glance.

"Do we plot to kill your enemies now?" Oleg asked when they got to the room. It was a forgettable place but very reminiscent of a Holiday Inn back home. Shane put on the coffeemaker and then headed to the bathroom.

"First, I shower. Then maybe eat something. Then sleep."

"This leaves little time for plots," Oleg pointed out.

"Let's use this time to recuperate. All the killing can wait a day."

The big ghost stared at him with narrowed eyes. He was too large for the doorways, and his head passed through them as he followed Shane into the bathroom.

"You are not a warrior? A soldier?" Oleg asked.

"Retired," Shane said, turning on the water in the shower to let it warm up before he got in. Oleg beamed and laughed.

"Retired! Like Oleg! I see it in you, but you turn away from it now. You have become a sage. A wise man!"

It was Shane's turn to laugh as he stripped off his shirt.

"No one's ever accused me of being a wise man."

"A wise man only kills when he needs to kill," Oleg suggested. It was not a traditional definition of wisdom by any means, but for someone like Oleg, it seemed reasonable.

"Going to need a few minutes to myself if you don't mind," Shane said. The big ghost shrugged and left, and Shane got into the shower. After so long living under the stars, nearly drowning in rivers, and being covered in the filth and bugs of Vakovia, hot water was a welcome experience that he reveled in.

Oleg was on the bed when Shane got out and showed no sign of moving. He stood over the big man, a towel wrapped around him, and stared down at the ghost until he finally moved of his own volition.

"Is a mattress comfortable? I never slept on one," he asked.

"Much better than dirt," Shane answered. He sat down and turned on the TV.

Oleg was enamored with television as Shane flipped through channels until he found some local news. He sat through weather and international items before the story turned to Peter Zemba.

Security camera and cell phone footage of the firefight in Seeburg played while a reporter detailed Peter Zemba's miraculous escape and the police hunt for Colonel Copland and the other Reapers, all of whom were dead.

Shane had to laugh at the report. He knew the cops were working with the Reapers, the army, and Janosik, but the media needed to make someone look like the villain.

"That's you," Oleg said, pointing at the TV.

Shane's face was included in a rundown of the wanted criminals, right alongside Copland. He grunted, hoping the hotel clerk hadn't gotten that good of a look at him. He wondered how long his face had been in the media. The police had it, and that was to be expected. Everyone having it was another matter.

No one on the way into town had even looked at him suspiciously. The weight loss, the filth, and the hat might have been a good enough disguise. If not, there was nothing to be done about it. The cat was out of the bag. He'd just have to continue to stay low. If anyone wanted to kill him tomorrow, he'd deal with it then.

Chapter 12
WANTED

"They're coming to kill you," Oleg said, roughly shaking Shane awake. It was still early, the window was dark, and the hotel was silent.

"What?" Shane asked. He blinked, trying to clear bleary vision in the darkness of the room and understand what Oleg was trying to explain.

"Outside. The vehicles with the rotating blue lights and men with guns have arrived. There are many of them."

"Police," Shane stated. His disguise had not been as effective as he had hoped. The clerk at the front desk had a hell of a poker face.

"Yes, police. They are here. There might be too many to kill. For you, anyway."

Shane cursed and got out of the bed, shouldering his pack, and heading for the door.

"Not interested in killing police today," he told the ghost.

He popped his head into the hallway to see if the coast was clear and narrowly missed being seen by a police officer exiting the stairwell. The exits were probably covered. He couldn't even get to the roof if they were already on the stairs.

"That won't work," he said, locking the door and setting the deadbolt in place. "Window."

Oleg went with him to the window and they both looked out at the world below. He was on the second floor, not too high, but higher than he'd wanted to jump from. He could see police cars at the end of an alley to his left, but none were down below, only dumpsters. If he had more time, he'd use the rope in his pack, maybe extend it with a sheet from the bed so he could reach the ground, but the police were already closing in.

"Are you a good jumper?" Oleg asked. It was about thirty feet to the alley below, which was flat pavement.

"Not that good," Shane said. There wasn't even a ledge to stand on outside. If he jumped, then he might perform a miracle, or he might break his ankle.

"Oleg will do it," the ghost suggested.

"You can jump to the moon and back; doesn't help me much," Shane pointed out.

"No. Oleg will jump you."

The two stared at each other in silence. Shane heard footsteps outside the room. Muffled, trying to be quiet, but definitely at the door.

"What the hell does that mean?" Shane whispered.

"You can destroy a ghost. You break them. You can hold on to Oleg. Quickly."

Oleg knelt and Shane stared at the ghost's wide, hairy back.

"Jesus," he muttered, shaking his head.

The doorknob turned as the main lock clicked, unlocked with a key from the outside. Only the deadbolt would hold them back now. He had seconds to spare.

Shane cursed silently at the indignity of the idea and wrapped his arms around the ghost's thick neck. Carl would have found amusement in the scene. Eloise too, for that matter.

Most of Oleg's body passed through the wall unencumbered but he angled himself to pass Shane through the window like threading a needle. He stepped out of the hotel room into the air and dropped to the alley below with Shane on his back.

He hit the ground without a sound and the vibration Shane felt was less like a sudden blow and more like someone braking too quickly in a car. He felt his insides heave and then settle.

"Good plan," Oleg said as Shane released him and slid down his back.

"That way is safer."

The ghost pointed away from the police. Shane nodded and they ran down the alley.

It took less than five minutes for sirens to fill the night. The police had retreated to the streets after not finding him in his room. Shane and Oleg had only traveled a couple of blocks.

They ducked down an alley between buildings and came out on the other side in time to see a blue light flash and a siren blare. Shane cursed and took a sharp right, running down a busy street as a police car gave chase.

"Here," a ghost yelled, standing at an alley between a restaurant and a variety store. Oleg went first and Shane followed. A door opened in the side of the variety store, but no one was there. Oleg entered, and Shane followed. A ghost with no eyes waited on the inside and closed the door after them. The lock clicked loudly, and they ran through the rear of the store to another door on the far side and into a different alley.

A different ghost pushed a dumpster next to a seafood market sideways, blocking the alley from the view on the street. Sirens echoed near and far, but spirits continued to block Shane from view and open doors to let him pass.

"One more block then right. A parking lot behind the spice shop," an alley ghost said. Shane kept running and didn't reply. He took the right and saw the parking lot.

"Silver car," another ghost by the entrance said, drifting past Shane and heading toward a park.

The silver car was parked at the spice shop entrance. The door was unlocked, and the keys were on the seat. Shane wasted no time, getting in the driver's seat and starting it up.

Oleg forced himself into the passenger seat. It vanished under his bulk and Shane couldn't see out the window. He ignored it and left the lot, driving as inconspicuously as possible.

"We should leave the city," Oleg suggested. Shane laughed and nodded.

"In retrospect, it might not have been the smartest idea to come here," he agreed. He passed police cars, pulling to the side to let them speed past just as other cars on the street were doing, going with the flow, and not drawing suspicion. They would probably not have had time to set up a blockade yet, so getting out of town would be relatively easy.

The police sirens wailed in all directions, but Shane stayed on his path to leave town, choosing the same street on which he'd walked to get to the hotel. A black SUV passed in the other direction and Shane glanced at the windows on the way by, catching a blood-soaked face staring back at him.

The spectral asset in the rear of the car opened his mouth but Shane could not hear what it was saying. If it hadn't recognized Shane, it had certainly seen the mass that was Oleg in the passenger seat.

Shane's foot hit the gas hard as the SUV spun a fast U-turn behind him.

"I think that vehicle is chasing us," Oleg observed, looking over his shoulder. Shane said nothing and weaved through traffic, staying on his original path.

A pair of police cars appeared on the road ahead, and Shane cursed loudly, taking a sharp left down a narrow cobblestone street. Ghosts watched him pass but could offer little aid during a car chase.

He raced around Mostava's oldest buildings, avoiding other cars and whipping down side streets. Another black SUV appeared, nearly spinning out after he passed it but correcting the fishtail and giving chase with the police.

Options became more sparse as additional police joined the pursuit, some cutting off streets ahead of Shane and forcing him to take alternate routes. He didn't know the city and did not know where else he could turn. Soon enough, he would have nowhere to go.

A sharp left led him down another narrow, cobblestone street. A ghost leaped in front of the car, and Shane had no way to avoid it. He plowed into it, and the spirit dropped back into the rear of the car, catching itself on the backseat and becoming a passenger.

The ghost was a thin and dirty man wearing a fur-collared leather jacket. He bore a long, angry scar from one side of his throat to the other where someone had nearly cut his head off from the looks of things.

"You drive a bit like a maniac, friend," the ghost said with a grin. He had a Czech accent but spoke English. Shane thought for a moment he was with the Reapers, but the ghost seemed content to just be hitching a ride.

"I'm not looking for passengers," Shane said, taking another hard right.

"But you do need an escape, huh? Turn right again and head for the river."

Shane looked at Oleg, who looked back at their new companion.

"Who are you?" Oleg asked.

"Radek," the ghost said. "Radek Dorn. I can get you out of here, but it will be tricky. You probably won't like it."

"Does it look like I like this?" Shane asked. He took another right and drove straight. In the distance, he could see the river he and Oleg had observed from the orchard before their arrival. "Where to now?"

"The Yesenk Bridge. You see there?" Radek asked, pointing left. Shane nodded and turned.

"Then where?" he asked.

"Nowhere," Radek replied. "You drive off the bridge."

Shane looked at Oleg again. The big ghost laughed.

"We go off the bridge?"

"Into the river," Radek confirmed. "Trust me."

"Trust you?" Shane asked. The bridge was approaching quickly. It was an old, stone bridge, something probably built a few hundred years before Shane was born that was originally designed for horses.

He was trailed by a string of police cars, close to a dozen now, and a pair of Reaper SUVs. He had come to the end of his options. Trust the random spirit from nowhere or get taken by the Reapers again. It wasn't much of a choice.

"Do you have a better plan?" the Czech asked. He knew Shane didn't.

"Where on the bridge?" Shane asked.

"Middle is probably most dramatic," Radek said. "But anywhere is fine."

Shane rolled down the front windows. He turned sharply onto the bridge, sideswiping a car in the other lane, and then floored it. The police were only yards behind him. On the far side of the bridge, there were more flashing lights cutting off his potential means of escape once he crossed over. The noose had been pulled tight; they were just waiting to watch Shane dance at the end of it.

"Trust me," Radek said again.

Shane cursed and spun the wheel. The front end of the car crashed through the stone wall bordering the bridge and sprayed rubble into the water. Shane was rocked in his seat, nearly smashing his head on the steering wheel before the airbags deployed. He snapped back as the front end hit the water and then freed himself from the seatbelt as the car began to sink.

"Now what?" Shane asked as the car filled with water.

"Now you try not to die," Radek told him.

CHAPTER 13
LOSSES

The ghost stood at the window, looking out over the city. The hole in his back passed straight through to the other side, the result of a powerful rifle round. It had entered through his chest, and the exit wound was bigger than a fist.

Blood dripped from the edge of his thick, wool uniform coat. It hit the floor with a steady tapping sound. The blood would never pool because it could not exist apart from the ghost. It lasted long enough to hit the floor, splatter, and then vanish just as a second drop fell. Over and over, ticking away like a morbid metronome. The ghost could stand still for a thousand years, and the drops would never stop or slow or go silent.

Major Emmett Fitzsimmons sat at the plain, mostly empty desk he'd been given and looked out at the skyline through the hole in the ghost's back. He could see the gaudy new buildings that had sprung up over the past five years, out of place in an aged city brimming with poverty and death.

His spectral asset, Cuddy, had once been a Continental Marine. His green uniform was stained nearly black down his back from the wound that had killed him all those years ago. Some soldier had shot the man point-blank and blown his back to shreds, tearing through most of his heart at the same time. If one got close enough—and Fitzsimmons had—they could see about a third of the muscle still twitching in his chest, one of the chambers still pumping blood.

Cuddy had been an unremarkable man in life. Fitzsimmons had gone out of his way to look up the Marine's service record. He was a corporal who had died at the Battle of Trenton during the Revolutionary War. He claimed he had served under General Washington, but Fitzsimmons could find no evidence.

The ghost had only served for a year before he was gunned down. He had no commendations, no record of admirable or distinguished service, nothing. He was a name on a page. His life had amounted to one document that confirmed he had, in fact, once been alive.

If he had a family, a job, a home, anything, all of it had been misplaced. Fitzsimmons had never asked the ghost about it, and Cuddy had not volunteered any information.

For another two hundred and fifty years after his death, he had remained a Marine. He wore the uniform because he had no choice, and he acted the part because it was what he knew. He never talked about his life before the Marines, and Fitzsimmons didn't care. Their partnership wasn't a friendship. They were soldiers. They had duties, and that was all. If either had wanted the other to be a friend, they probably would not have worked as partners.

What Fitzsimmons liked about Cuddy was that he didn't mince words. He didn't speak at all unless he needed to. He wasn't coy or mysterious, he didn't brood, and he didn't waste time. He was efficient and reliable and emotionless. Not cold, not hateful, he just was. He was like a machine. The major wished more soldiers were like him.

A knock came at the door of the sparse office he'd been afforded in Ravjek. Fitzsimmons had never been to the country before and only needed a small space to work. Men working for President Janosik had found him and the company office space in a building downtown. They were not to wear military uniforms in the country, and they were not to use the name Silvershore or Reaper Company. No one needed to know who they were.

"Come in," Fitzsimmons said.

One of the privates entered and held out a folder.

"Message for you, sir. From Mostova."

Fitzsimmons nodded, and the private left. He'd never liked the name Reaper Company the way most of the men seemed to revel in it. He thought it was silly and childish. Something a teenage boy would think of. Of course, most of the soldiers seemed to have a case of arrested development, so that fit. He didn't know why Colonel Copland had allowed it. But Copland was dead now, so it didn't matter.

Fitzsimmons opened the file and read the sheet of paper.

"Target drove off a bridge into the Tyvus River," he read.

Cuddy did not turn from the window.

"Dead?" the Marine asked.

"Salvage efforts are underway."

"He probably escaped," the ghost suggested.

"We'll operate under that assumption until facts dictate otherwise," Fitzsimmons agreed.

He did not know Shane Ryan, but he had seen the man's service record. He had been a good soldier. Smart and capable. Good with languages. And, it seemed, skilled at dealing with the dead. That had not been part of any official files.

Fitzsimmons had never heard of someone who could hurt ghosts. He and others in the company could see them, and speak with them, and it was a hell of a logistical feat to gather troops into an endeavor like that. To not only find those who fit the bill but were cut out for the work. It was one in a hundred thousand soldiers if that. And then Ryan showed up, and he could break them open like walnuts.

The whole point of Silvershore was that they could do the impossible and be unstoppable. No one could stop a ghost. But now, someone could. It flew in the face of decades of work, careful recruitment, planning, and reputation building.

If a man like Ryan could show up and cause an international incident by himself, then the Company wasn't worth a spit. They would lose every client they had. And since Copland was dead, Fitzsimmons was the one who'd pay for it. He couldn't allow it.

"It is a good distraction. He's tied up our men with a fruitless search that he knows must be undertaken. No matter how many we assign to the task, it's men who can't be in the field," Cuddy observed.

"But it must be undertaken," Fitzsimmons said, repeating the ghost's words.

The major did not intend to ever have a field command in the Reapers. He had retired, in part, to avoid the command structure of being a soldier. He didn't want to lead men or be responsible for their lives and actions. He wanted money and privacy. He wanted to finish jobs quickly and quietly and be done with them.

Colonel Copland had been too enamored with aping military structure. He loved being the commanding officer and having the power to sway markets, political discourse, and whole cultural movements with a single order. Spectral assets could change the world in an afternoon, and no one would know what happened or why. They could destroy Fortune 500 companies, assassinate world leaders, or set off weapons of mass destruction. The Reapers were like gods on the earth in Copland's mind.

Fitzsimmons saw them as resources. They could make a million dollars for less than a week's work. He could send Cuddy to kill a man, never see that man's face, and be rich. He'd spend the whole time reading the paper. That was the draw for him. And Shane Ryan had ruined it all.

Fitzsimmons had never liked Copland, or his grisly spectral asset. The two of them lacked critical thinking skills. They were like animals, driven by urges and whims and emotions. Nothing practical or sensible. But the military liked a man with fiery passion who could survive despite those shortcomings. So, Copland became a colonel and his experience was considered valuable and laudable. When he retired and joined the company, he was considered an asset and not a liability. No one said you had to be smart to be important, the entirety of human history was a testament to that.

"This man is becoming a real nuisance," Fitzsimmons said. Cuddy kept his gaze fixed out of the window.

"Copland couldn't contain him. Perhaps it's best to cut our losses and let him go."

"No," Fitzsimmons said flatly. "He needs to die."

"Then the men need to stop trying to capture him."

"Client's orders," the major pointed out. President Janosik wanted Shane Ryan alive. He was a tiny tyrant in his little world and liked to flex those muscles. He'd want Ryan paraded before him so he could use him as a tool to show what a good President he was by capturing and executing the wanted criminal. Such a waste of time and money.

"A good dog must obey," Cuddy mused.

Fitzsimmons grunted, and the ghost finally turned away from the window. The ghost's face was broad and pale. He had two days' worth of stubble and just the beginning of what looked like jowls. He was puffy, and not the sort of man who would have cut an intimidating figure on the field of battle. Things had been different back in the day.

"The company is yours now. We should finish our business here and go home. This city is… unpleasant."

"It's morbid," Fitzsimmons agreed. "Never seen so many ghosts walking around. But the company is not mine."

"It's under your command," Cuddy said. He was not wrong, but he was not right. He knew that, too.

"My direct command. Here, and now."

"If Shane Ryan dies, no one will belabor the point of who committed the act. The man leaped into a river to escape. He's as good as dead already."

Fitzsimmons considered Cuddy's words carefully. There was something to be said for a target's recklessness. They could chase the man around for the next month or more. They'd had him once, and he'd escaped. Almost had him again earlier, and he'd destroyed a ninety-million-dollar helicopter.

"Maybe it's best if Ryan doesn't make it to Ravjek alive," Fitzsimmons said.

"It would be more efficient," Cuddy agreed.

"With Vakovian police after him, there's every reason to believe anyone could kill him at any time. I can worry about the paperwork later."

"War shouldn't be about paperwork," the ghost said. He was right. Fitzsimmons hated the red tape, and the meetings and rules and business Copland had thrust upon him by dying. Fitzsimmons had never wanted to run the show. He was not supposed to be in command. But if they put him there, then he'd do things the way he wanted. And what he wanted was to end things quickly.

Fitzsimmons pressed a button on the old-style office phone on his desk. A knock came at the door a moment later, and the private who had delivered the message returned.

"Send a message to all units. Target is to be eliminated on sight. Report back with confirmation. Until then, proceed at own discretion."

The private nodded and left the room. Fitzsimmons sighed and leaned back in his chair. It was not comfortable and wobbled on one side, but he didn't care. He'd be done with the temporary office soon enough. He could return to the U.S. and someone else could worry about Silvershore and whatever business they wanted to run a million miles from home.

"Will we leave when Shane Ryan is dead?" Cuddy asked. He'd never explicitly said that he disliked traveling, but he always seemed more comfortable in America. Cuddy was not a complainer, but he didn't like wasting time, either.

"Let's get Shane Ryan dead first and see what happens," Fitzsimmons said.

CHAPTER 14
Escaping Death

Shane took his pack and pushed out of the window of the car and escaped into the murky, brown river water. The current pulled at him, and there was only the faintest sense of up and down. The sky somewhere above provided a contrast in the light and nothing more.

Oleg grabbed Shane's arm under the water and dragged him along. The big ghost ran across the bottom of the river, unaffected by water speed, temperature, or even opacity. He saw what he needed to see and moved as though he were still on land. Shane dragged behind him like a fishing lure.

He held his breath, hoping the ghost had some concept of how long a living person could last underwater. He didn't want to rise to the surface yet, however. Whatever Radek Dorn's plan was, they needed to get far enough from the bridge so that the police and Reapers, and most importantly the spectral assets who had surely followed them into the water, couldn't see them.

Oleg dragged him against the current into a darker part of the river that must have been under the bridge. Shane felt a pressure in his lungs, slowly growing more and more prominent, but he didn't fight Oleg or try to surface. Instead, he maintained focus and calm, holding his breath for as long as possible.

The big ghost grabbed Shane with another hand and pushed him against an unseen destination. Shane felt around the edges of something metal with his hands. It was an entrance of some kind, hidden from light, with the swift current pulling at it.

Shane moved inside while Oleg gave him a push from behind. They were in full darkness now. A second freezing hand in the dark latched onto his wrist and pulled forward and upward.

His lungs strained and pain blossomed in his chest, but he kicked his legs and continued in the direction he was being pulled. Then water receded around his head, and he was suddenly in the open air.

There was no light by which to see anything. Shane floated, treading water, in a current that was not moving as swiftly as the river but still pulled him back the way he'd come. He reached out in the dark and felt corrugated metal on a wall, curved all the way up over his head. He was in a pipe of some kind. He was back in a Vakovian sewer.

"Be quick or be dead," Radek spoke in the dark. Shane struggled forward, unable to see where he was going but agreeing that moving was better than waiting for the Reapers to catch up.

"Where are we?" he asked.

"Other side of the bridge. The Tyvus floods in the spring. Used to damage everything along the river for miles until they expanded these drains years ago. You can travel much of Mostova underground. People live down here, farther from the river, where it stays relatively dry."

"Living in the tunnels in a city full of the dead. Sounds familiar," Shane said.

He'd experienced some of that in the Boston subway and didn't want to endure it again. But it had proven helpful in a pinch. The tunnels were also not as unpleasant as those he'd traveled in Ravjek. Maybe the river kept clean water flowing through them and prevented a buildup of sewage and filth. He was thankful they barely smelled. The ghosts would not have cared or even known.

Radek led them deeper into the tunnels, and the water level dropped lower and lower as they went. He talked about his years in Mostova, his life as a paratrooper, and how he once had plans to retire to a vineyard and be drunk on wine for the rest of his life, but it never happened. Soon, they were only ankle-deep, and the ghost slowed their progress.

"We can surface soon, but I can only take you so far once you are able to get away."

"You should bring him with us," Oleg suggested. "It is good to have fellowship."

"Fellowship," Shane said. "Sure."

He could still barely see either ghost in the darkness. The only light that reached the tunnel came from rarely placed drain covers, many of which didn't even exit onto streets but into basements.

"Up here," Radek said, directing Shane to a ladder that led up into the darkness.

"Where are we?" he asked.

"This is an apartment building," Radek said. "The basement. No one is there, and the door is locked from the inside."

Shane climbed the rickety ladder. Things moved under and around his hands, and he realized cockroaches were scuttling across the dark ladder. He ignored them until he reached the top, where he had to use his shoulder to loosen the cover to get out. The heavy slab of metal scraped across the floor as he moved it enough to get some leverage and then pushed the rest of the way with his hands.

The basement was as dark as the sewer had been, but Radek pulled a chain, and a dim bulb hanging from a wire hummed to life.

Bed frames and boxes lined one wall of the basement, and empty shelves covered the other. The place smelled of dirt and age, and was too damp to be dusty. Radek pointed out a table under an old pegboard that held a handful of rusty tools.

"Here," he said, pointing to a drawer. Shane pulled it open and looked at the assorted junk inside. Old fuses, mismatched screws, a tobacco tin, and, finally, a silver pin featuring a mostly faded coat of arms. He could feel the coolness before his fingers even touched it. It was Radek's haunted item.

Shane looked at the ghost. They'd barely even met, but it had been an intense, if brief, period of getting to know one another. He slipped the pin into his pocket.

"Now what?"

"Speed is our friend. The police are probably going to dredge the river, but your other enemies will already be looking elsewhere when they see no body in the car," Radek said.

The ghost was not wrong. The spectral assets would have reported him missing within minutes. He was not certain how far the apartment was from the river, but Radek had only given them a short time to make an escape, so wasting it would be foolish.

"I hear you are heading north," Radek said. The basement door led them to a hallway full of pipes and more moisture. Tiny, arrow-slit windows covered in a frosted material let in faint, gray light near the ceiling.

"Good thing it's not a secret mission," Shane said.

"I know of the demon you hunt," the ghost replied. He led them to a set of concrete stairs and then up to another door. "I have heard of it for many years now. It devours spirits."

"Nothing devours Oleg," the big ghost replied.

"I suspect not," Radek agreed.

Shane opened the door, and they were in an apartment hallway. Ugly, green paint made it look like a hospital from the seventies, and the carpet squished underfoot. An exit on their left led to a parking lot.

"I will find us a vehicle. You should remain out of sight. The hallway should be safe," Radek suggested.

"I will look for these Reapers," Oleg added.

"Got it," Shane said.

The paratrooper and Oleg left the building together, leaving Shane alone in the vaguely musty hallway. Radek was big on timing, so he expected a quick turnaround. Mostova was no longer welcoming, but the addition of another set of hands and an ally who could think on his feet wasn't a bad tradeoff.

Shane kept back from the door so no one passing by would catch a glimpse. Across the hall, a door labeled with a brass number "2" creaked very quietly. Shane glanced at the door, expecting a resident to come out, but no one did. The door was open but just barely, a tiny crack indicating it hadn't been closed properly whenever someone passed through last.

The door creaked again, opening inward, just an inch. There were no sounds from in the apartment and no reason for the door to be creaking open on its own.

"Something you need?" Shane asked. No one answered. He could see no one, living or dead, near the door but there could have been on the other side. In Vakovia, neither was a surprise.

The door creaked open further, allowing a partial glimpse of the darkened apartment within. The windows must have been covered, as the interior was as dark as the cellar had been. Shane was reminded of the ancient ghost outside of Zevna who told him about the ghosts they shunned. They stayed in the dark because they were not welcome in the light. They didn't follow the rules. They didn't want peace.

Shane stayed where he was in the hall. The apartment door moved, inch by inch, until it was fully open. The apartment was fully dark within, and he could only make out the outlines of what might have waited inside. A hallway led to a doorway on the left and also straight back, deeper into a vast blackness. A room, maybe, but it was hard to tell.

The doorway to the left was the only clear thing, illuminated by light from the hall. Nothing moved.

"Help me," a small voice asked from the shadows. Shane said nothing. "Please, help me."

He adjusted the pack over his shoulder and glanced at the exit. There was no sign of Radek or Oleg yet, but it had only been minutes.

A faint hint of movement brought Shane's attention back to the apartment. A shape emerged from the doorway on the left of the hall.

Midway up the doorframe, something small and pale slipped around the edge. Fingers eased around the corner. Bone-white, the nails were caked in a thick and dark substance. A single hand eased itself slowly into view. The fingers twitched and separated as the hand slid along the plain, ugly, green wall toward the door that had opened itself.

Shane watched, waiting to see what would happen next. The palm of the hand was flat on the wall, and he could make out a scarred wrist as something new appeared. Red hair, chunky and clumped with what might have been grease or mud, preceded the edge of a face. A single eye appeared, the rest hidden by the doorframe. One eye, silver-blue and ringed in blood red, stared with a wide pupil at Shane. The hand shuddered, and the nails clicked on the wall.

Plump, red lips that looked stained around the edges by a rash pulled back into a smile. Half a smile for half a face. The teeth were yellowed. More dark, oily residue was caked between each one and around the pale gums.

"Help me," the voice said again. It wasn't coming from the ghost whose partial face was visible but something else deeper in the apartment. The thing watching him was silent. The eye was locked on Shane, and the red lips quivered with expectation.

Shane could make out faint movements from the darkness at the end of the hall. Bodies in the shadows, several together, low to the ground as though crawling. They were silhouettes in the dark, impossible to see, more impressions than anything else. They writhed, maybe in pain, or maybe something else.

Shane sighed audibly and approached the door.

"I am helping you," he said. His hand closed over the knob, and he pulled the door shut as Radek reappeared at the exit. The paratrooper looked at the apartment and shook his head.

"You shouldn't go in there."

"Didn't," Shane pointed out. "Thought you said this place was safe."

Radek grinned and stayed where he was.

"I said, 'The hallway should be safe.' That's a different thing. But I found a car. We should go now."

The door behind Shane began to creak open again as he left. He didn't bother to look back to see if the spirit was watching him go.

Chapter 15
Demon Hunters

Radek had found an SUV with tinted windows, suitable to hide Shane from view and also Oleg, who would otherwise stand out like a sore thumb to any ghost they passed.

"They are already searching. But slow and unfocused. They do not know where to look," Oleg said when he rejoined the others. "There is only one vehicle, and they are heading away."

The police were still heavily focused on dredging the river, and one of the Reaper SUVs stayed while the second searched. They left Mostova without a hitch.

They were miles from the city when Shane felt they were finally able to relax a little. He wanted a cigarette.

Water dripped from the pack in his pocket. They were crushed and saturated and completely unsmokable. The ones in his bag were the same way. He threw them out the window in frustration.

There was no time to stop, and he was out of money anyway except for a few dollars they'd need for gas. He forced smoking out of his mind as he continued north.

Seeing Vakovia from the road again was a nice change of pace from the seemingly endless hiking. No need for ghost guides and no hiding from helicopters. Just the road and dark windows.

They passed a few black SUVs, but Shane could not tell if they were Reapers or just travelers with similar taste. He stayed at the speed limit and didn't do anything suspicious, avoiding notice as a result. Every vehicle passed them without incident, and none followed.

Radek and Oleg gave directions as best they could, but neither had traveled the country much since most of the roads had been paved, and a number of towns and landmarks they knew in life had changed their names or been destroyed. The general direction was enough to get them in the ballpark, though, and Shane wasn't going to worry about precise locations until he had to.

Day faded to night, and Shane continued the drive. The spirits of Vakovia were out in full force as they drove past. Radek and Oleg watched them with a quiet sort of awe. It was unlikely either of them had ever traveled so much after their death that they could see just how many of the dead roamed the land.

"Is this normal?" Radek asked sometime after midnight.

"What?" Shane asked.

"The dead. Is it like this everywhere?"

Shane followed the ghost's gaze to a field. There were a few dozen spirits near the roadside, spaced out like they were waiting to cross, but they were not. They were just watching.

"No," Shane answered. "Vakovia is unusual."

"The dead are not like this where you come from?" Oleg asked.

"Not in most places. You can find them everywhere, of course. But outside, like this? No. Far fewer where I come from. Some cemeteries are not even this active."

"Death was too busy here," Oleg said. "Like a young man who thinks he can hold his drink but cannot. He overindulges and makes himself look a fool."

"Death got drunk," Shane mused. "That's as good an explanation as any."

"Death got overwhelmed," Radek suggested. "I remember the forest during the war. I fell through the trees to the sound of gunfire and explosions and screams. More screams than I had ever heard. Corpses on top of corpses, the forest floor slick with blood-red mud."

He was silent for a moment, and only the hum of the SUV's engine filled the gap. The ghost chuckled then, but it was not a happy sound.

"The man who slit my throat was bathed in it from head to toe. I thought he was the devil come to drag me to hell. He smiled and screamed in a fury as that blade bit into my flesh. And then he was gone. Off to kill more. How could Death hope to keep up with such madness? I wonder if he left the whole country behind and washed his hands of it."

Shane had no answer for either ghost. He knew from time spent with Carl and the others that dying did not bring answers. The gateway between life and death was metaphorical at best. No enlightenment came from dying. No one explained the meaning of life as you crossed over.

Sometimes the dead returned as spirits, and sometimes they did not. Shane knew nothing more about it and neither, it seemed, did anyone else. Not the living, and not the dead.

He wondered how true that was. People looked at Shane like he was impossible. They said he was the man who could kill ghosts. He would correct their word usage, insisting that you couldn't kill what was already dead, just destroy it. But it was skirting the issue of his uniqueness.

The ancient ghost at Zevna had said there was another like him. And at the Iron Tournament, he had seen others who could fight spirits. Maybe some knew the mysteries of death. Like Shane, maybe they just preferred to keep to themselves. What a burden it must be to understand why some people return as ghosts. He didn't know if he would have told others if he understood it. It could only lead to more questions and expectations.

It was close to two in the morning when Oleg saw a sign on the roadside that caught his eye.

"This is where we need to go," the ghost said.

Shane followed the sign's directions and took the turn toward a place called Hannec. The closer they got, the more desolate the landscape became. There was still an abundance of trees. In fact, they were entering some of the densest forestlands Shane had seen since coming to Vakovia.

But the dead were growing sparse.

Groups of spirits and wandering fields of the dead dwindled to a handful of walkers, and that faded to a single spirit every so often. When they reached the borders of the small town called Hannec, there were no ghosts at all. Shane had not kept track, but he was willing to bet there had been very few ghosts for the final mile before they reached the town.

"Hannec," Oleg said softly. "This was where I was supposed to be."

"Home sweet home, huh?" Shane said, driving slowly into the town.

There were a handful of houses, each with a small garden out front or along the side of the structure. Some had pens with goats or chickens or pigs, and the largest property sat before a sprawling field of corn.

There were no shops in Hannec, not even a church, which Shane found unusual. Just the houses, clumped in a tight area that covered a few blocks. Nearly all were built of dark stones that looked as though they had been cobbled together a few hundred years earlier, held in place by thick, white mortar.

No ghosts wandered the few narrow roads that crisscrossed Hannec. There were no people awake, either. Only one home had a light on, obscured by drapes, and the rest were as dark as the night.

"If it wasn't for the livestock, I'd assume this was a ghost town," Shane said.

"Just the opposite, I think," Radek said. "The dead aren't welcome here."

"This is where the demon lives?" Shane asked.

"No," Oleg answered. "This is Hannec. The demon is not here. But it is close."

Shane pulled over next to a big maple tree and turned off the engine. Whatever they were there to do, they would need some guidance. Radek and Oleg seemed to only know the demon by reputation. Shane needed something more concrete. At least a place to start looking if Hannec wasn't the source.

The three left the vehicle and stepped out into the cool night. Crickets sang and toads croaked, and the sounds of the nearby forest were like a symphony Shane had not heard in a long time.

"Where do we start?" he asked. The ancient ghost had told him the final guide would have some kind of relevant information. Unless the whisper network of the dead failed, they had to know he was there.

"There," a voice answered. A ghost stood in the center of the road, several yards from the three of them, back the way they had come. It was a woman, old and frail, the left side of her face consumed by a large, purple bruise. The ghost pointed to a road out of town, up a hill, and into the trees. Shane looked but could see nothing.

"What's there?" he asked, approaching the spirit.

"The demon, they call it. It's not from Hell, and don't let it trick you into thinking it is. Just a man. Or was, once. But bad. Soiled to the soul. That is where you will find it."

"Can you show us where to go?" Shane asked. The woman shook her head.

"I go no further than this. This is the only reason the thing hasn't taken me like it has taken so many others. I cannot reach it, and it cannot reach me. The distance of a stone's throw. But if it knew I was here, now, it might devour me like it devoured so many others."

"You're stretched to the edge of where you can go," Shane said. Her haunted item, a mile away, gave her a buffer against the demon. Their territories overlapped, but not enough that it could take her.

"In the morning, ask for Yakov. He will take you where you need to go. You must be wary. This demon is brutal. It will not give you quarter."

The woman turned from them and walked away, down the road and into the woods, vanishing into the night.

"We wait for the morning?" Oleg asked.

"Probably more polite than knocking on doors," Shane said. They needed one final guide. But they'd be at their destination then, and that was worth something. They would track the so-called demon, destroy it, and then…

Shane had no idea what came next. The ghosts had promised to help him leave Vakovia, and that was what he wanted. But he had no passport and no money. Getting back to America was going to take help that the dead couldn't provide. And Reaper Company was not going to stop chasing him just because he crossed a border.

Despite his many days crossing the country, Shane had not spent a lot of time working on a strategy. He had no information on which to build one. Where was he going when he left Vakovia? Who could he get to help him? How far would the Reapers go to get him back? Too many questions and no real answers meant he could only spin his wheels.

The demon, the ghost of the north, that was a real problem with a simple solution. All ghosts were basically the same, whether people feared them, loved them, or didn't even realize they existed. He could destroy it and fix a problem for someone who had offered to help him, and there was some comfort in that.

Shane returned to the SUV to get some sleep. He would wait for whoever Yakov was, and in the morning, he'd go find a Vakovian demon and crush its skull.

Chapter 16
The Cemetery of St. Jude Thaddeus

If Shane didn't know better, he would have assumed Yakov was a ghost. The man looked worse than a lot of the dead Shane had seen. He looked worse than Radek, and Radek's throat was slit.

Yakov, who had once worked in a Vakovian mine near the Ukrainian border, was like a skeleton covered in liver spots and the odd scab. He claimed to be just over one hundred years old, and Shane believed him.

When Oleg woke Shane before sunrise, Yakov and two other men were coming out to meet him. The other two, who were likely in their eighties, were nearly as frail. They wore simple wool garments, and their feet were adorned with homemade leather slippers.

"The departed have sent you here," Yakov said. His eyes were watery and only half open, but he spoke to Shane as well as Oleg and Radek, fully capable of seeing them. He showed no fear.

"I was told you have a problem with a ghost."

"The demon of St. Jude Thaddeus. It is a plague on our land," one of the other men said.

"It eats the dead," the third added.

"And the living?" Shane asked.

"The demon is fickle," Yakov said, his voice crackling with the sound of fluid in his throat. "Some have died by the demon's hand. Others have fled. Others, it leaves alone. We few have stayed to warn away those who might venture too close to the cemetery, and to preserve what once was."

"It shuns the light, but it can appear in it. We will take you to the cemetery as the sun rises, and you may battle the beast in its lair," the second man said.

Shane glanced at Oleg and Radek and then nodded. He'd taken on more than his fair share of ghosts before, but none had a build-up like this one. He was almost afraid to see it, not because of how much everyone had hyped it up, but because he knew it could never live up to the reputation.

The three old men moved incredibly slowly, leading Shane and the two ghosts up a dirt path in the direction the old woman's spirit had pointed out the night before. The route couldn't even be considered a road, though it might have been at one time. Now, it was a footpath cut through weeds and shrubs alongside the forest.

When they got close enough, Shane could make out the remnants of fencing and a gate, as well as a structure. Among the weeds, a handful of tombstones rose high enough to be seen over the greenery. The cemetery had long ago been reclaimed by nature.

There was a church on the land, the reason there was none in the town, but it was half-collapsed and overgrown. Another decade or so, and it would be rubble. The cemetery of St. Jude Thaddeus was on its last legs.

"A spirit near the town of Zevna told me a man came here to fight this ghost a long time ago," Shane said. Yakov nodded and coughed, then spit something into the dirt.

"A spirit warrior, yes. He failed."

Shane had hoped for some more details, but none were forthcoming.

The trio of elders led them to the collapsed gate of the cemetery but stopped short of entering the grounds.

"This place is no longer hallowed. It is tainted and desecrated. You will find the demon here. It will not remain hidden long once it is aware of your presence."

"What happens when we destroy it?" Oleg asked. Yakov smiled at the ghost.

"No one has done such a thing, so who is to say?" he asked.

"Not a bad point," Radek conceded.

"Have there been strangers in the area recently?" Shane asked. "Black SUVs or helicopters flying overhead?"

"Men came," the second old man said. "A week ago. In a dark vehicle. They traveled with the departed, and they were armed. We thought it was you at first."

"They searched the village. Even here, at the cemetery, but the demon did not show itself to them. They left and did not return," the third man added.

Shane nodded. The Reapers had covered a lot of the north already, then. It meant they knew where the place was, though. They could come back.

"One more thing," Shane said as the old men seemed ready to part ways. "Your demon here, you've seen it before?"

"Many times," Yakov stated.

"Does it speak? Has it said what it wants?"

Yakov hummed and nodded, the gesture giving him a slight tremor.

"It wants to be Death," the old man said. "To take that gift away from all others until only it remains."

The old men turned and left, and Shane stood at the cemetery entrance with the two spirits.

"Sounds arrogant," Radek remarked.

"Heard it before," Shane said. Some ghosts had lofty, fantastic goals of sowing chaos on a grand scale. It was easy to dismiss as madness, and in a way, it probably was. But if nothing else, Vakovia had made him think about the nature of death and those who returned as ghosts.

Someone like Carl had picked up very much where they left off. He had died in the Anderson house and returned, fully aware that he was dead, how he had died, and the implications thereof.

It was not impossible to imagine some ghosts did not have things so easy. They returned and had to assume there was a reason. Returned from the dead, effectively immortal, no longer needing food or water or sleep. Invisible to the living and wielding the power to alter their perception and kill without being stopped. What would an already fragile psyche think of something like that? Being dead might seem very much like being an all-powerful force of nature.

"How do you hunt spirits?" Oleg asked as they crossed the threshold onto the cemetery grounds.

It had been years since Shane had seen a cemetery that had no spirits roaming about. He wasn't even sure he could remember such a thing. There seemed to always be at least one, even if it kept to itself quietly in the shadows. St. Jude Thaddeus was the opposite of what it should have been. And it was no small plot of land.

Though the growth of weeds and even some smaller trees obscured much of the property, the borders were still fairly well-defined, thanks to the ancient fence. At some point, it had been a well-used cemetery, and there were hundreds of dead there. Not a soul still remained. All were consumed by the so-called demon.

"I usually just look around for them. Most ghosts don't feel the need to hide. Comes from never being seen," Shane explained. Ghosts only seemed to hide from the perspective of the living who couldn't see a spirit until the ghost manifested. The rest tended to loiter.

Oleg seemed unimpressed, and Shane shrugged.

"It's not hunting in the traditional sense," he added.

"No, it is not," Oleg agreed.

They walked through knee-high grass and around old, crumbling stones. Some were too damaged to read, and some bore dates and symbols rather than names.

"These are all two hundred years old or more," Shane said. He had not seen a single more recent date. The ruined church on the land had to be at least that old.

He hadn't thought to ask the old men how long the demon had been in the cemetery, but it seemed like no one had used the place in more than two centuries. Maybe other parts had more recent graves, but he didn't think he was likely to find any.

"Not so old," Oleg said.

"Time is relative," Radek added. "I read that once in a book."

"Very philosophical," Shane said.

Yakov had told them that the ghost would come for them when it was aware of their presence. The cemetery would have countless places for a ghost to hide, but the most obvious choice was the church.

Shane trudged through the weeds toward the collapsed building. The morning dew saturated his clothes and set a chill into his bones. Birds in the nearby woods started in on their early morning songs, and everything had a peaceful serenity to it that flew in the face of the demon Shane had been warned about.

Only the north-facing wall of the church remained fully upright and intact. Something had happened to the southern wall and brought down most of the other two walls alongside it. There was no indication of what might have brought on the destruction, but the amount of growth and the aged look of everything suggested it happened a very long time ago.

As much as Shane could see, the interior of the church had not been disturbed. Neither locals nor bandits had seen fit to loot the building. A large, ornate golden cross still stood in the center, miraculously untouched by the roof that had caved in around it. There were candelabras, a thurible, and one still-pristine stained-glass window in the north wall depicting the archangel Gabriel with this trumpet.

Shane stood on the stone steps that led to the half-obscured entrance. If the ghost was anywhere, it was in the church. But going inside would mean climbing over timbers and stones that hadn't been touched in more than a century and were set precariously at best. There was still a quarter of a roof on the building and no telling what could make the north wall collapse.

"Looks unsafe," Radek said. "I'll go."

"I will stay to keep you safe," Oleg proclaimed, patting Shane on the shoulder with a large, icy hand.

Radek slipped into the church, gliding over wood and stone, and disturbing none of it. He covered the interior quickly, unrushed but maybe not as thoroughly as Shane would have.

He slowed when he reached the rubble of the south wall, stopping to inspect the timbers around the transept. After a moment, he ducked out of sight and then vanished completely.

Shane and Oleg waited for his return. The sun rose higher above the trees, and the light of day fully washed across the cemetery. Radek then rose from the ground, rushing from the church back to Shane's side.

"It's like Hell down there," he said, pointing back the way he had come. "I have never seen anything like it."

"What did you see?" Oleg asked.

Radek gestured furtively at all corners of the cemetery.

"It's… dead. Death. A thousand. A million dead. More than I have ever seen. Bones as far as the eye can see."

"The bones of the dead?" Oleg asked, gesturing to one of the tombstones. Radek shook his head.

"You should see for yourself. There are stairs and a hidden entrance. They say you are chasing down a demon. Everywhere ahead of us is the kingdom of a demon. Come, I'll show you."

Chapter 17
The Demon's Kingdom

Oleg and Radek cleared some of the roof timbers aside. Sections of the roof collapsed about them and would have crushed Shane had he been standing close enough. Instead, he remained in the grass while the ghosts cleared a path to a panel in the southern transept that led down a flight of stairs.

Shane took one of the candles from the old church and lit it using a lighter that surprisingly still worked, before heading down wooden steps into the darkness. Each step creaked and whined like a dying thing on his way down, but they held his weight.

The space below the church was cold and stale. The smell was something Shane had never experienced. Age and decay to be sure, but something more that he couldn't put a finger on. It was not a pleasant odor.

Light from the candle flickered and danced and sent shadows over the stone and wood-reinforced walls until he reached the bottom. The room at the base of the steps was small, a vestibule, with a hallway branching from it.

Shane held the candle high. A circle of skulls was embedded in the wall opposite the stairs to greet anyone who entered. Taller than a man, each skull had been set into a depression carved from the stone to fit it. The circle rose higher than Shane and spread wider than he could reach from side to side with both arms outstretched. Inside, a cross made of skulls three across fit the space.

To the left, the light of the candle flickered enticingly at the entrance to a hallway. What lay beyond was more bones. Not just skulls, but ribs, spines, pelvic bones, fingers, femurs, tibias, fibulas, and every other bone in the human body. They were arranged along the walls from floor to ceiling.

Shane stood at the hall entrance. As far as the light touched, it sent shadows dancing through the bone art set into the walls.

"It's an ossuary," he said.

"There are many rooms," Radek said. "Empty save for the bones."

Shane reached out to one of the nearest skulls. A hole punctured it above the eye. The weapon had left gouges in the bone, straight and deep. Something sharp and metal had pierced the person's skull.

Other bones bore signs of trauma as well. A partial rib cage had a wound the size of a thumb that left a star-shaped cut between two ribs. An arrow. They had died in battle, or at least many of them had.

"This place is probably older than our demon," Shane said. "These dead are ancient."

They walked the hall together, with Oleg hunched low to fit the space. As Radek had said, the hallway led to more chambers. Like the entrance vestibule, each was decorated with the bones of the dead. The sculptor had chosen specific bones to make patterns. Crosses were prominent, but so were images that resembled the sun, with finger bones extended out like rays around a sphere made of skulls. A river flowed below, depicted in waves made with bones from arms and ribs.

Each chamber was different. Candelabras and sconces were positioned to allow the rooms to be viewed when the candles were lit, and Shane used his candle to ignite the wicks and see what each room held.

The intricacy was unparalleled, and the time taken to finish it all must have been remarkable. Years, Shane guessed. Most remarkable of all was the scale. There were chambers and more chambers, a maze carved below the cemetery. Radek had not been wrong when he described the number. Thousands of corpses were used to construct the ossuary. Tens of thousands.

There was no way the town of Hannec could have supplied so many dead even if it had been founded a thousand years ago. There must have been another supply of bodies, a great war or terrible famine or something else that had killed a lot of people.

"There have been wars here," Radek said as they traveled the bone-filled halls. "This land was ruled by conquerors again and again and again. A hundred battles were fought in Vakovia between armies of soldiers that never had a home under this sky."

A swift current of chilled air blew through the hall and threatened to snuff the candle. It carried a musty, rank smell from somewhere in the dark.

"I think we've got someone's attention," Shane said, shielding the flame from the breeze.

They headed into the next chamber, where Shane lit several ancient candles set into wall sconces then set his in one of two candelabras. The chamber was round, so there were no corners untouched by light. Only shadows that danced within the bones.

"We make a stand here?" Oleg asked.

"Good a place as any," Shane decided. If the ghost was coming, he would rather let it come to him than be caught off-guard in the hallway or chase it down. Yakov and the men of the village made it seem as though the ghost was not one to play coy. It knew someone was in the ossuary. It would be on its way.

"Oleg will find this demon first. You wait here," the ghost volunteered.

Shane caught his hairy arm before he could leave.

"This ghost has been here for at least a couple hundred years. It has, by all accounts, eaten every other ghost within a one-mile radius."

"No one eats Oleg," the brute said. Shane patted the spirit on the arm.

"Until we know what it is and what it does, let's stick together. Just in case."

Oleg grunted but did as Shane asked and remained by his side. The confidence of the dead was second to none, but overconfidence was never good. Oleg, like spectral assets, was certain no one could hurt him. Shane knew better.

The breeze blew into the chamber with them and swirled among the candles. One went out, but the others remained lit.

Silence filled the space with an almost oppressive presence. The breeze stopped abruptly. Shane could feel the tension building and kept his eyes locked on the entrance to the chamber.

A shriek cut through the stillness. It was garbled and forced. It rumbled and squelched, and Shane barely had time to register it before the ghost burst from the hallway.

It clambered into the room on all fours along the wall rather than running on the floor. Shane could understand why they called it a demon.

The ghost had lost any sign of whether it had been a man or a woman in life. Its body was a livid, angry red from head to toe and adorned with loose, swaying flesh that hung in thick, pale curls where it had peeled away from muscles but not torn off.

Some of the body was blistered, especially on its back, where a massive, head-sized blister was plumped full of a thick, yellow liquid beneath a bubble of translucent flesh.

"In God's name…" Radek muttered, staring wide-eyed at the ghost as it scuttled along the bone walls.

Shane had seen similar wounds but never to such an extent, never full body like they appeared on the demon. Whoever they were, they had been boiled alive, cooked, and rendered nearly unrecognizable as human.

Every inch of exposed skin was either as red as raw meat or rolled up and pale white like rice paper as it peeled away. Liquid sloshed in bubbles and openings across its body. It squelched as it moved, but it was so much faster than it seemed like it should have been.

In seconds, it had climbed the wall to the ceiling and launched itself at the biggest target.

Oleg caught the demon, and red hands dug fingers into his arms. The ghost howled, and a gout of steaming liquid belched forth into Oleg's face, blinding him.

As Oleg cried out, more in surprise than anything, the demon dove for his throat, gnashing its teeth.

Shane's fist hit the demon's jaw before it could clamp down. The boiled ghost flesh felt as solid as any other Shane had fought, and the ghost's jaw snapped shut. Oleg only needed that one moment to grip the ghost and hurl it across the room in the direction it had come.

"You fight like a coward," the big Viking said, wiping spectral vomit from his eyes and flinging it off of his fingers.

The demon did not pause or reply or plan. It landed where Oleg had thrown it and bounded back, this time for Radek. The paratrooper scowled and kicked at the red ghost. The demon caught his leg and bit into his calf muscle, causing him to cry out in frustration.

It was not clear if the ghost they called the demon was capable of rational thought any longer. It was like an animal, a starved and caged beast that could only lash out.

It had no fear or hesitation. It was like the men in the village had said. It was death, and it was focused not on Shane at all but on the ghosts. It wanted whatever power they could give it.

Shane tried to pull the ghost from Radek's legs, but it had latched on with fingernails and teeth. Radek was punching it in the side of its face as it began to chew.

"Get your hands in here fast," Shane said to Oleg as he crouched next to the red-skinned nightmare. He thrust his hand between the ghost's jaws and Radek's leg, putting his hand in jeopardy as he gripped the ghost's lower jaw and pulled.

Oleg forced his hand into the other side of its mouth, and the demon spasmed and jerked but Shane refused to let go. The ghost would not cooperate, so Shane pulled harder. The jaw snapped, and the ghost vomited again.

Boiling liquid splashed over Radek's leg and Shane's hand. He cursed and pulled away, feeling the heat searing into his flesh. Oleg cried out as the demon reached out blindly and took hold of an ear, tearing it from the bigger ghost's head and tossing it aside like trash.

With its jaw hanging low and crooked, the demon retreated and faced Shane. He could see it clearly now for the first time. The eyes in its head had been cooked until they bloated and turned white. Whatever hair had been on its scalp must have peeled away with the lost flesh. All of its features were distorted, warped by Shane's assault but mostly the damage done before death. Its head was like a skull adorned with clumps of red meat, disjointed and ugly.

It didn't look like it should be as fast as it was, and it didn't fight like a man. No opponent, living or dead, would stand a chance if they were not prepared. Even then, it seemed to have no fear or caution.

The demon ran at them again, spraying vomit like a weapon to force them back. Oleg slammed a fist into the ghost's face, breaking teeth in the upper jaw, and it still fought him. Ghostly nails raked through the Viking's flesh, cutting runnels through it while Oleg kept deflecting. One finger hooked into Oleg's eye and pulled the organ from the Viking's face.

Shane tore the ghost away from Oleg and forced it to the ground, straddling it to keep it in one place. The blister on its back exploded, gushing vile-smelling fluid across the floor. Shane gagged but was forced to remain focused as the sloppy, sagging arms and legs lashed out while the spirit writhed beneath him, nearly bucking him off.

He caught a hand as it went for his eyes and bent fingers back, breaking them. Radek's booted foot stepped on the demon's head, pushing it to the side a moment before it vomited another torrent of boiling liquid that would have shot into Shane's face.

Shane held fast to the ghost's wrists while Oleg took up a position behind him, holding down the legs.

"Do it," Shane said, looking up at Radek. The paratrooper grimaced and turned his head as he pushed his boot down. The demon never spoke a word. Never even communicated. Shane turned his face away as its skull crunched under Radek's boot. The blast rattled bones loose from the ossuary wall and snuffed every candle in the room.

CHAPTER 18
RETURN OF THE DEAD

Stone crumbled and walls collapsed. Bones spilled out, rolling over and over on one another and overwhelming Shane. The rattle became deafening, and in the dark, it was impossible for him to tell what was happening.

The rush of movement, the dry and jagged bones, soon became overwhelming. More and more weight piled on top of him, and he tried to pull himself free. Every movement seemed to loosen more bones, burying him deeper and deeper.

"Imagine this," Oleg said, his voice coming from the blackness at Shane's side. "You spend all this time hunting the dead, and you are killed by skeletons."

Shane didn't answer. The weight of stone and bone on his back pressed him hard to the floor and forced the air from his lungs. The deluge had slowed, but the weight was unbearable. He was going to suffocate.

Things continued to shift, and he felt something on his wrist, cold and firm.

"It is not right to die in the middle of your victory," Oleg continued. He pulled Shane hard as the debris on his back was forced away. The pressure lessened, and soon, he could breathe again.

Oleg pulled him straight up through a pile of rubble and then pushed him or let go, it was hard to tell in the dark. He fell back to flat ground, cluttered with only a few errant bones, and then got to his feet.

"Here," Radek said. Something else touched Shane's hand, firm and waxy. A candle.

Shane pulled out his lighter and lit it. He was in the hall again. The chamber in which they had fought the demon had caved in. Oleg was waist-deep in bones and grinning despite his missing eye.

"We are demon slayers!" he bellowed. Radek clapped Shane on the back.

"I had no doubt," Radek said.

Shane nodded, still catching his breath. All things being equal, the job went down more quickly than he had expected. Not that the ghost didn't live up to the hype, but Oleg and Radek had made it easier to handle than it would have been if he had fought solo.

More bits fell from the chamber ceiling, and Shane backed away. The whole underground could have been compromised, and he had no intention of contributing to the body count of the ossuary.

"Maybe we should head topside," Shane suggested. He turned away from the chamber and was stopped by the presence of another ghost.

"Who is that?" Radek asked. Shane did not know.

The ghost was a man with a medium complexion. He wore a helmet that came to a point on the top and was bordered by flaps that looked like dirty wool. He stood silently in the hall, watching Shane and Radek and soon Oleg.

"That is an Eastern warrior," Oleg pointed out. "They fought well on horses."

"A Mongol?" Shane asked. He had seen something like the armor the ghost wore in a museum before, but the empire had died out nearly eight hundred years ago.

"Mongols? That's before my time," Radek said. "Is that what they looked like?"

Another ghost appeared in the hall, walking toward them. The armor he wore was completely different, featuring bits of plate and what looked like a red skirt.

"An Ottoman," Oleg said. The new ghost walked right up to the group and then continued down the hall as though Shane and his companions were not there.

"Ottomans and Mongols would have been here centuries ago. And not at the same time," Shane said.

He reached out a hand and touched one of the skulls on the wall, feeling the texture of a groove sliced into the bone. That was why there were so many bones in the ossuary. Hannec was built on a battleground, one that had been used more than once in the past.

There were mountains to the north, and the south contained a lot of scrublands. Hannec and the cemetery were on fertile ground. Maybe an ancient city had made use of the land. Something had drawn warriors there in great numbers. Many might have survived, but it was clear many had not.

With the demon destroyed, the dead that had hidden from it were returning. Like the dead across much of Vakovia, they showed little interest in the living.

Shane approached the Mongol, and the ghost's gaze did not alter. He was not looking at Shane, he was looking down the hallway, now focused on nothing. They passed him and returned to the vestibule.

"This could be a good place to hole up for a while and plan," Shane said, looking up the stairs at the way out.

It was a maze underground, well hidden from view, and the entrance could be disguised under the rubble from the church. The ghosts were not the talking sort, so even if the Reapers returned with their spectral assets, no one was likely to give away Shane's secrets. He'd have time to come up with a strategy for his next move.

Escaping Vakovia was an unclear goal. He needed a destination and a plan for how to turn that into a way home without getting killed. Poland and Slovakia were options. He wasn't sure how far from Czechia he was, but that might have been on the table as well.

"You're staying for a while, then?" Radek asked.

"Have to," Shane replied. "Reapers aren't letting me hop on a plane and go home without a fight."

"So… plan to escape or plan to destroy your enemies?" Oleg said.

"Both," Shane answered. He didn't think he could leave without fighting, and it might make it worse to try. If he evened the playing field a little, he might have better results. On the other hand, the Reapers could strafe the cemetery if they discovered him and burn everyone's bones to ash. He would need to proceed with caution.

"Then we should make this place as unwelcoming for your enemies as we can," the big ghost suggested.

Shane headed to the surface. The sun was warm, and the sky was clear. The cemetery, once desolate save for the birds and weeds, was now a swarm of activity.

The dead had returned in numbers. Dozens wandered through the grass. Shane watched the swell of spirits drift slowly but peacefully. They did not acknowledge one another any more than they had acknowledged Shane.

There were clear factions among the dead. An army of Mongols had died nearby, as had the Ottomans. Others that Oleg claimed were Russian, some Hussite, some Bavarian, and a smattering of soldiers who wore armor from places like Poland, Hungary, and even a few French.

"How many battles?" Shane asked.

"At least eight," Oleg guessed.

"All in this same place?" Radek asked.

"These Polish warriors," Oleg began, "died here a hundred years ago. The Mongols? Eight hundred. The Turks? Two hundred. All for that."

He pointed his finger toward the forest. Radek glanced at Shane and shrugged.

"What was in the woods?" Shane asked.

"The forest city of Bek. An outpost of the Holy Roman Empire. A waypoint for traders and travelers. Great center of commerce. Hard to attack but hard to defend. Not the most valued spot, but important to disrupt trade. It was how politicians fought wars. Take a place like Bek to control commerce and cripple your enemy."

"Did anyone ever take it?" Shane asked.

"Many times. Just as Vakovia has known many masters, so did Bek. The Mongols, the Turks, the Poles, the Bavarians. Everyone took and lost the city. The dead are proof. Success or failure, all the time."

"Did you have any idea that so many people died for it?" Shane asked.

"No," Oleg admitted. "At least now they are free of the demon and can be at peace. It is some small reward."

They returned to Hannec and told Yakov and his companions of their success. For all the buildup to the fight, the reaction was fairly reserved. Not that Shane sought praise, but the old man nodded and said that it was good. He offered Shane food, however, and that was more than he could have hoped for.

"You may stay here in the village for as long as you like," Yakov added.

Shane turned him down. He didn't want to be in town if and when the Reapers returned. Better to stay in the ossuary for as long as he was in the area. It was safer for him and the old man.

He moved their stolen hidden SUV, driving it closer to the cemetery, and hiding it off-road among the trees and under cover so it couldn't be seen from overhead or by any casual observer. The goal was to remove any trace of himself from the area.

Oleg and Radek both knew survival skills, albeit different kinds. They were still adept at setting traps, though, and understood how to make use of their surroundings.

In Ravjek, Shane had used homemade traps to take out Reapers, and the forest around St. Jude's offered a better location to set up more complex ones. When the Reapers came—and they would come eventually—he would be ready for them.

Oleg was adept at digging holes with great speed, and Radek weaved bark from trees into tough rope that could hold substantial weight.

They lined pits with sharp sticks, set man-sized snares, and rigged several heavy stumps up in the branches with coverage over half a mile.

Nothing large lived in the forest, mostly birds and rodents, and the men of the village were too old to venture there. No one had reason to be in the woods. Nothing should have been able to spring the traps until the time was right.

Shane and the others had been in the cemetery for just less than a week when the opportunity presented itself deep in the woods as they were setting traps a couple of miles from their base. The sound of helicopter blades from the south echoed among the trees.

"They're patrolling," Shane said. It sounded low like those inside were vainly trying to get a view into the woods. Below the cover of the canopy, no one flying above would see him or the ghosts. "They'll follow with ground patrols if they stick to their pattern."

"If you want to wait, that is," Radek said, staring up beyond the treetops.

"Meaning what?" Shane asked.

The former paratrooper shrugged, his eyes still fixed on the sky.

"Just that there are a lot of ways to take down a helicopter if you know what you're doing."

The ghost lowered his head and looked at Shane. The rhythmic sound of the beating blades was loud and incessant, reverberating through the woods.

"Do you know what you're doing?" Shane asked.

Radek grinned. The ghost set his hands on the closest tree and began to scale it rapidly. His fingers pierced into the tree and found purchase. He climbed it faster than Shane could climb a flight of stairs.

The wind from the helicopter tore at the treetops. Radek reached the top of the canopy just as the chopper flew overhead. The ghost jumped from the treetop and grabbed hold of the landing gear before the helicopter flew out of Shane's field of vision.

"He can defeat this machine?" Oleg asked.

"Seems to think so," Shane replied.

The Reapers had not brought the other King Stallion but a smaller European model that would have seated a half-dozen at most. Still, it was an asset they wouldn't have wanted to lose.

Seconds passed, and the sound of the helicopter changed drastically. The engine struggled, and the acoustics of the blades warbled. Yards away, Radek dropped through the trees to the forest floor, laughing like a madman.

Trees exploded behind him as he ran back toward Shane and Oleg. Metal groaned and wood snapped. The helicopter crashed to the ground, snapping the tail as it fell.

It landed hard and brought a tree down on top of itself, further crushing the cockpit. Two others fell alongside it and then, within a minute, the forest was silent. There was no huge explosion, but the destruction was still brutal.

"Let's go find the spectral assets," Shane said. Some of the Reapers might have survived the crash, but if they had, they'd be in bad shape. Shane and the ghosts had just declared war on Reaper Company.

Chapter 19
WAR

"Who the hell are you?"

The ghost walked from the wreck of the helicopter and met Oleg and Radek. He was slightly taller than Radek and dressed in a disheveled, damaged suit. His face was scarred with what looked like road rash, and he was unable to close his left eye as a result.

"We are with him," Radek said, pointing behind the ghost. He turned in time to see Shane kick out his knee.

The ghost dropped to the ground, and Oleg attacked in an instant. One stomp with his foot, and he crushed the ghost's head into the forest floor, exploding it and knocking himself backward.

A second spectral asset climbed from the ruined chopper and Radek darted forward. He dragged the ghost to the ground before Shane even saw its face, twisting its neck around and tearing its head from its body.

"You guys got money on this?" Shane asked as the second ghost came apart, rocking the crashed helicopter with the force of the blast.

"Not yet," Radek said, looking at Oleg.

"A bet?" the big ghost laughed. "Oleg would take all of your money and your children's money. And their children's money."

"Worry about it later. Let's get some distance," Shane replied with a laugh.

The three of them took what they could from the helicopter, taking armor, weapons, and some gear. Still no cigarettes. Shane carried as much as he could manage and Radek followed behind, covering any sign of his tracks to throw off the rest of the Reapers when they arrived.

Days passed. A convoy of Reapers arrived north of Hannec. One group went to the village and tossed the houses but could find no sign of Shane. The others scouted the woods. Six men died in traps by the time the group fell back.

Shane and the ghosts had placed traps in three locations to make it harder to pinpoint their base of operations. The first was within range of the cemetery, the second was near the river, and the third was at the ruins of Bek.

The forest city had not been a city in the last century. It had been obliterated and now was a patch in the woods lined with the stone remnants of walls and foundations. It reminded Shane of the ancient ruins that were sometimes unearthed in Central America. Places that didn't look like anything had ever been there until people started pulling back the weeds.

Reapers set off traps in all three locations. Shane stayed underground when they came so their thermal cameras would pick up nothing. His ghost companions sometimes wandered with the forest dead, slow and deliberate so they were indistinguishable from the Ottoman warriors, Mongols, or French who populated the woods. Almost no one knew of Radek or Oleg, and the few who may have seen them with Shane in Mostava probably hadn't gotten a good look. The system was working well.

It was Shane's sixth week on the run in Vakovia. He never imagined he'd be stranded for so long, but they were making progress against the Reapers despite the odds. One man, two ghosts, and a series of ancient survivalist traps had taken out at least two dozen of them since it began. And that didn't include Copland's men.

Things were going to get ugly soon, though. They sent a dozen Reapers in after the second helicopter crash. After the six who died in traps, three fled from the river site, and Shane took out the other three with Oleg and Radek.

Vultures circled the wreck of the chopper. Shane didn't know how much longer he'd have before he couldn't keep the cemetery base secret any longer. He also didn't know how many more Reapers the company had to spare.

Oleg had urged him to eat. Shane wasn't in the mood, but it was a reasonable suggestion. He had supplies in the ossuary. They headed down.

Shane used a lantern to light his way, and at the bottom of the steps, he stopped next to the stair post.

"Six weeks to the day," he said, looking at the marks in the wood.

"Could be worse," Radek told him from the dark.

"Could be," Shane agreed. He didn't want to make it a competition between himself and anyone who'd been stranded and hunted in a foreign land, though.

He turned around and raised the lantern. Shadows danced across the faces of a hundred skulls in the little vestibule at the base of the steps. Radek and Oleg waited at the entrance to the hallway that led into the depths of the ossuary.

"Six weeks," he said again as he followed them into the dark. Something scraped at the top of the stairs behind him, and he tensed, turning in time to see three objects clatter to the floor.

"Grenades!" he yelled, ducking into the hall with the ghosts.

The blast was concentrated in the enclosed space. The sound faded to an all-consuming ringing in seconds. Shane could hear nothing else. The ground shook, and debris fell on his back as smoke and dust filled the air.

"Are you alive?" Oleg asked, hoisting Shane roughly from the ground. The lantern was destroyed, and Shane couldn't see anything.

"Alive," Shane confirmed, his hearing slowly coming back as the ringing faded.

"The entrance is destroyed," Radek pointed out. "We have been discovered."

"Move," Shane ordered. He urged the ghosts onward and began to run blindly down the tunnels. The Reapers had gotten the drop on them somehow, but they were not going to stop at blowing the entrance.

"They are not following," Oleg pointed out.

"Don't need to if they blow the cemetery," Shane told him, using his hands to feel along the walls.

"Here," Radek said, forcing a candle into his hands.

Shane lit the candle as they ran, following the maze of tunnels through the underground. Radek had discovered a second entrance to the ossuary near Hannec, but the route meandered around and around.

"Leaving so soon?" someone asked from back the way they had come.

Shane looked back, and a ghost in a T-shirt and jeans was in the hall behind him. He was an average-looking man and would not have stood out at all if not for the fact he was American in a two-hundred-year-old Vakovian cemetery.

"Considering it," Shane answered. If they stopped to fight, the Reapers would have time to blow up the cemetery on his head. He had to keep moving. He ran.

Another ghost appeared from one of the bone chambers, this one military. He went for Shane, but Oleg caught him first, slamming the spectral asset into a wall and then wrenching his head from his shoulders.

"You got sold out, Ryan," the ghost behind him said with a laugh. "Got a couple of friendlies in a place called Oba to drop a dime on you and your little hero play up here. Fighting a demon? Really?"

The ghost laughed again, and a third spirit attacked from ahead. Radek and Oleg took this one out together while Shane continued at a steady pace, shielding the light of his candle as he ran.

"Told 'em I was a good friend of yours, and they told me everything," the ghost behind them continued. "It was kind of pathetic."

"I'm really happy for you," Shane shouted back. "This'll be a cool story to tell your friends at your next campfire."

"Do you even know who I am, Ryan?" the ghost called out. There was enough distance between them now that Shane couldn't see the spirit any longer. He was not running after them, and Shane was happy to let him keep flapping his jaws if that distracted him from catching them or giving away their position.

"Some asshole who talks too much?" Shane suggested. Oleg laughed loudly.

"Mick Guilfoy," the ghost said as if it meant something.

"Great," Shane said back, shrugging at the look he got from Radek.

"They gave me the gas chamber, Ryan. Thirteen murders that they knew of. You know how many more I killed? Dozens. They didn't even solve a fifth of the ones I did."

"Wow. Bravo. Gold star for you," Shane shouted.

"I'm going to take my time with you, Ryan. I'm going to make you scream."

"Keep talking; I'm almost there," Shane replied.

"Maybe I'll just tell them to bomb this whole place and bury you with your jokes," Mick told him.

"If you don't think you can handle me yourself, do what you gotta do," Shane said. They were still five minutes from the exit. The tunnel circled the cemetery before doubling back to Hannec. He needed to keep the ghost engaged.

"You're not going to be hard to handle," Mick said, his voice echoing down the halls. "You're not going to be anything."

"I can twist off his head," Oleg offered.

"No. If his item is still intact, they know he's still down here. If they're rigging this place to explode, they'll hold off to see if he succeeds," Shane replied quietly.

"No funny comebacks?" Mick shouted in the distance.

"Was just laughing with my friends here about your misplaced confidence. Copland dead, two dozen Reapers dead. You guys keep throwing bodies at me and failing miserably."

Now it was Mick's turn to laugh.

"You don't think that's intentional?" he asked.

Shane raised an eyebrow. Reapers volunteering to die did not sound intentional.

"Money is still changing hands, Ryan. No one cares about these Reapers any more than they care about you. At this point, it's about two things: cash and vendettas. You made it personal to someone at the top of the food chain. They don't care if everyone in Vakovia has to die. You'll be dead, and if anyone's left alive, they'll go home, and next week, we'll have forgotten this place and you and everything that happened here."

"Personal, huh?" Shane asked.

"Count on it," Mick said. His voice sounded muffled, and Shane wondered what had happened until they rounded a bend and found the ghost waiting ahead of them. He'd passed through the walls to cut them off.

"Now how about—" Mick began. Oleg slammed a fist into the ghost's face and then threw him on the ground, using his foot to keep Mick's body down while he yanked off his head with both hands. The ghost exploded and caused Oleg to stumble, but he kept his balance.

"He was giving us information," Shane pointed out.

"He wastes time," Oleg countered.

Something rumbled in the distance, and Shane cursed.

"Charges," he said. They had rigged St Jude Thaddeus with C4. The whole cemetery would be consumed.

Shane ran, and the ghosts ran with him even though they could have easily escaped by heading to the surface. Not that they were in much danger to begin with. The C4 charges went off sequentially across the cemetery. The explosions grew closer and closer as Shane tossed the candle and ran through the dark as fast as his legs would carry him.

The final round of explosives went off, and the earth shook as though taken by a quake. Shane was still running, down a tunnel that left the cemetery grounds and led toward the village of Hannec. The Reapers had not found the second entrance and were not aware of how far the ossuary spread.

Stale air and dust thundered down the tunnel and swept Shane up in the blast as the cemetery caved in on the ossuary and buried the bone tunnels and chambers.

They reached the exit, a metal door obscured behind mossy rocks beyond the edge of Hannec, and paused.

"I'll go for the SUV if it's clear," Shane told the ghosts. "If not, we make for the river."

Oleg opened the door, and the sound of rifles being raised rattled around the boulders.

A dozen Reapers and their spectral assets had staked out the rear entrance. Only one, a soldier in a green beret, hadn't bothered to raise his weapon.

"Shane Ryan," the man said. "What a pest you have proven to be."

Chapter 20
Man Down

Shane's hands were raised. Behind him, Oleg and Radek were motionless but wary. The man in the green beret smiled and held up a twisted piece of metal.

"I see you dispatched Mick," the man said, tossing the warped item at Shane's feet. At least one Reaper had learned not to keep their asset's haunted item close at hand when they sent it after Shane.

"He talked too much," Shane said. The man in the beret nodded.

"I'll give you that. He was a loudmouth. Bit of a creep, too, if I'm being honest. Beggars can't be choosers, though."

"I bet," Shane said, scanning the faces of the soldiers and spirits around him. Too many to try anything out of turn.

"I'm sorry, I'm being rude. Captain Reg Banner. I've heard so much about you these past few weeks, I feel like we're old friends," the man said.

"Captain Banner. Green Beret, I have to assume," Shane said.

"Yes. Not just a fashion statement," Banner confirmed.

"I'll shove that hat down your throat," Oleg growled.

Banner smiled tersely, and Shane shook his head.

"Not this time," he said to the ghost.

"Oleg does not lose," came the reply.

"If you want to be destroyed, big fella, just say the word," Banner offered.

Oleg growled again.

"The word." He pushed past Shane and swiped at Banner, knocking the beret from the man's head as the captain ducked and fell back.

Ghosts were on Oleg from all sides like hyenas on prey. They leaped on his back, went for his arms and legs, and two took him on directly.

Shane moved to help, and the barrel of a Reaper's gun pushed into his cheek. He stopped, hands up, while Oleg raged and beat at the ghosts.

"Oleg, stop!" Shane shouted.

The Viking would not listen. He crushed the head of the first spirit easily, and one of the Reapers screamed as something in his pocket exploded. A spray of blood doused Shane as the man's leg separated at the hip.

"I told you to drop those anchors, soldiers!" Banner yelled.

The other Reapers began discarding packages of various sizes, some in boxes, others in cloth, while Oleg continued to take on the assets. The big ghost roared as two ghosts pulled the muscle from the back of his left leg, tearing it off and throwing it behind them.

Radek said nothing as he watched, his face a mask of pure anger. He wanted to help, Shane could see, but knew it would be fruitless.

Two more assets were squashed by the big ghost's rage, and then three working together broke his right arm. They twisted and wrenched until the joint came away at the elbow.

Unable to walk and lacking his dominant arm, Oleg was like an injured bear. He swatted at anything that came near with his good arm, propped up on one knee, but he was slow to turn, and the spectral assets took advantage.

Oleg made no sound as one of the ghosts latched onto his neck. The others worked his left arm, struggling as a unit to break it. His body still bucked and thrashed as they piled on, kicking, punching, and even biting whatever bits of Oleg they could reach.

They rolled on the ground together, Oleg and six spectral assets, all that remained of the group. There was no strategy, no technique, just frenzy. They were animals fighting for scraps. They were beasts with no sense or humanity.

"You fight like cowards," Oleg bellowed and then laughed. Shane watched him sink his teeth into one of the ghost's necks and jerk at it until he tore it off, destroying another of them. He kept laughing until they managed to pull his head apart.

The explosive force was like a bomb. The five surviving spectral assets were launched in all directions, and the Reapers were all bowled over.

Shane fell with them but recovered faster. He took the rifle from the man who had it trained on him and drove the butt into the fallen man's face, breaking his nose and knocking him out. Blood spurted and flowed freely as Shane pushed the man aside and turned the rifle in his grip, taking quick aim at the first thing he saw.

He shot the next man in the knee as he got to his feet. He was ready to take out another when he was forced to stop. A pistol cocked and fired right next to his head before he was even fully upright.

The sound was nearly deafening but Shane stopped, letting go of the rifle.

"Good boy," Banner said, pressing the still-warm barrel of the gun to Shane's face next to his eye. "Up nice and slow."

Shane got to his feet as the rest of the Reapers did so, save the two he'd taken out and the man who lost a leg.

"Hell boys, look at that. We had this man dead to rights, and he still crippled three of us with a dozen rifles trained on him. Now that is soldiering," Banner shouted to the others.

Someone began patting Shane down. After a moment, they found the silver pin that bound Radek's spirit.

"Say goodbye to your smarter friend," Banner said. He opened a lead-lined box, and another reaper dropped the pin inside.

"Shane—" Radek began. The box closed before he could finish, and the ghost was gone.

Banner came around to face Shane, gun still in hand. He kept it on Shane's flesh, tracing his cheekbone down to the jawline and then lowering it until it was on Shane's Adam's apple. They stared each other in the eye.

"Tell me you're done now," Banner instructed.

"You think I am?" Shane replied. The Green Beret pressed the barrel hard enough into Shane's throat to make him cough.

"I get it. You're not scared. I'm not here to make you scared. I'm just here to take you in. I've got orders that I'm free to kill you on sight, you know that? Use my discretion, it said. But I think it would be a lot more interesting to bring you back to Ravjek than to gun you down in a forest."

"How noble of you," Shane replied. Banner smiled.

"I don't know about that. I feel like things will get more exciting if everyone who wants you gone gets to see you face to face. I have to admit, I'm curious as hell. No one's even been able to tell me who you are or why you're here. You're just this… boogeyman, killing Reapers and ghosts like it's your job, and I want to know why. And I expect someone will pay me a lot of money when I show up with you, too."

Now it was Shane's turn to smile.

"Of course," he said. "It's always about the money."

"We're mercenaries, Ryan. It *is* always about the money."

Some of the other men laughed, and Banner's eyes shifted.

"Tie him up nice and tight. He's got more lives than a cat and has a knack for escaping," he said.

One of the Reapers pulled Shane's arms back roughly, and the familiar sound of a zip tie preceded his hands being forced together behind his back. They led him through Hannec and up the road toward the cemetery where they had parked their vehicles. They didn't get close enough to see St. Jude again, but they didn't need to. Shane could see the cloud of dust and smoke and the chasm they had created on the earth.

The ghosts had gathered around the edges of the sunken graveyard. They stood like spectators around a stadium, watching what was happening below. Death had not made them leave; a simple explosion wouldn't, either. They'd adapt, just like the dead of Vakovia always did.

Oleg's item had been put to rest in the cemetery. Now it was gone, and so was he. The Reapers couldn't do anything without causing destruction. It left a bitter taste in Shane's mouth.

He'd had his revenge on Copland for what had happened to his friend Davis Blakely. Things could have been square then. Should have been. But the Reapers were fast becoming some kind of twisted onion of atrocities and violations. Layer upon layer of reasons for Shane to destroy every one of them.

Banner led Shane to the nearest of the SUVs while another of the Reapers opened the back door. He pushed Shane's head down and helped him into the back then sat down next to him, gun still trained on him.

The Reapers dispersed to their various vehicles and drove out as a convoy, passing Hannec on the way back to the freeway that would lead them south to Ravjek.

Shane saw Yakov and the other old men outside of their houses as they drove past. The windows of the SUV were too dark for them to see him, but he had no doubt they knew what had happened. The whisper network of spirits had probably spread the word across Vakovia already, too. The demon was dead, but the Reapers had come for Shane Ryan.

"Any chance you're going to tell me why Fitzsimmons wants you dead so badly?" Banner asked.

"I don't even know who that is," Shane replied. The Green Beret stared at him for a moment, judging the answer, and finally chuckled.

"You're telling the truth, aren't you?"

"I came to Vakovia to find out why Davis Blakely died. I found out he was murdered by Colonel Copland. I took care of Copland and was ready to go home. Then you guys showed up. Now you know the whole story."

"Are you serious?" Banner asked. Shane met the man's stare. "So, this business with Janosik and Zemba, what was that?"

"Not my pig, not my farm," Shane told him.

Banner laughed again and shook his head.

"So, you're just a sucker. A fall guy to put on the news and take the blame?"

Shane watched him enjoy his laugh and waited until he was finished.

"Seems like your guy Mick knew more about this than you do," he pointed out. Banner went silent at that and adjusted the grip on his gun.

"Meaning?"

"He understood there had to be a reason why someone kept sending you guys out to die."

"No one sent us to die," Banner corrected. Shane shrugged.

"If you say so. How many of you died hunting me? My count was two dozen."

"Twenty-nine," Banner said flatly.

"More guys on that first chopper than I thought," Shane replied.

"You're saying someone wanted us to die? Reapers aren't in the business of dying," Banner pointed out.

"No, you're in the business of making money, and surely the money you're making will be spread evenly among the widows and family of the dead."

"Not buying it," Banner said. Shane shrugged again.

"Don't need to. Someone wants chaos in Vakovia, and they want Reapers in the middle of it. That was true before I even showed up. I'm no expert in the dynamics of international instability caused by special forces that use the dead as a weapon, but I think the demonstration works if you all live or die," Shane told him. Banner laughed again, but this was not a laugh of enjoyment.

"You're talking out of your ass, Ryan."

"Anyone pulling the strings can now show new potential clients how one person can blow up a pair of helicopters, usurp a foreign election, take out dozens of trained soldiers from across the spectrum of elite fighting forces, and on and on. If we're not on opposite sides, we're both just pieces on a game board, then we both played a perfect game for someone else who's probably getting a lot more out of this than either of us."

It was by no means a perfect theory, and much was genuinely stuff Shane had pulled out of thin air. But Shane had wondered for weeks why the Reapers seemed so bad at tracking and why their commanding officer was sending them after him piecemeal. It could have been poor leadership. Or maybe the real force behind the Reapers wanted a longer demonstration.

If Shane was lumped in with the Reapers, just like he had been on the local news, just another guy who can talk to ghosts, then they had put on a seriously impressive war games demonstration using Vakovia as a gameboard. They rigged it, to be sure, but it would give nice optics when selling Reapers to others like Janosik around the world. Look at how Reapers and their ghosts can track, kill, infiltrate, and more.

"Let's just see what happens when we get to Ravjek," Banner said.

"Can't wait," Shane replied. He didn't imagine anything good was going to happen.

CHAPTER 21
BEHIND ENEMY LINES

The drive back to Ravjek was long. Banner kept a close watch on Shane the entire time. There had been no opportunity for an escape or a distraction. Shane's hands were bound tightly, he was at gunpoint, and he could do nothing.

The SUV convoy rolled to a stop on the outskirts of the oldest part of Ravjek's downtown, alongside some Soviet-era office buildings. Shane was dragged from the back of the vehicle and into a drab, utilitarian building, and then walked up ten flights of stairs. Banner kept a gun in the small of his back the entire time.

No sound echoed through the halls, and no one passed the Reapers on their way up the stairs. It seemed like the building was abandoned. When they reached their destination, the office Shane was led to smelled old and unused. Mustard-colored carpet was underfoot, and creamy orange walls completed the sickly look.

Everything was empty and unused save for a single desk at which sat one man with a computer and a phone, a ghost leaning against the wall next to him, and a closed office behind him.

One of the Reapers knocked on the door.

"Come in," came the muffled reply from within.

The Reaper opened the door, and Banner ushered Shane in. The rest of the mercenaries and their spectral assets stayed outside.

The office was just as dull as the rest of the floor. Empty shelves lined the walls, and a single officer sat at the desk while a ghost in a green, continental Marines uniform stared out the window. The ghost didn't bother to turn around when the door opened.

"Target acquired, Major Fitzsimmons, sir," Banner said, and nothing more. The man at the desk, a little older than either Banner or Shane, looked from the captain to Shane and back.

"You brought him in?" Fitzsimmons said. The tone of his voice suggested that it was not according to plan.

"At my discretion, sir," Banner replied. There was clearly some tension between the two men, but Shane said nothing. Fitzsimmons was obviously the new commanding officer in Vakovia, but he was just a major. Copland had been getting running orders from someone, and surely, it hadn't been Fitzsimmons. The group was not technically military anymore, but Shane couldn't imagine a major running the show above Copland.

Fitzsimmons stood from behind his desk and adjusted his black sweater. He stepped out into the open and was slightly shorter than Shane, enough that he needed to crane his neck just a bit to make eye contact as he approached.

"Shane Ryan, you are a true pain in the ass, do you know that?" Fitzsimmons asked.

"I have heard words to that effect in the past," Shane answered. The other man didn't smile.

"Do you have any idea how much that CH-53K King Stallion you blew up costs?"

Shane raised an eyebrow. Of all the things he expected to hear from the head of Reaper Company, that was not it.

"Is it a lot?" he asked.

"That's a ninety-million-dollar asset, son," the major said. "And the second one you just destroyed? That was an A109. That was five million dollars. That's nearly one hundred million dollars in assets. Toss in the Silvershore HQ, and it's over one hundred million."

Shane turned his head so he could see Banner in his peripheral vision.

"Is this guy your accountant?" he asked.

Fitzsimmons' fist took Shane by surprise, digging into his gut with more force than Shane would have guessed the other man could muster. He doubled over, coughing as he pulled in air. Fitzsimmons stayed put.

"Point is, Ryan, we're running a business, and you really messed it up. If Colonel Copland had shot you the day he met you, things would have gone much more smoothly, but efficiency isn't everyone's strong suit."

"Yeah, that's true," Shane agreed, straightening up again.

"And now look at where we are. Captain Banner was kind enough to bring you back here, through the front doors, I imagine?" the major asked, looking over Shane's shoulder.

"Sir," Banner replied.

"So, you're on camera, and we can assume Zemba's people already have the footage and that your face, in our custody, will be all over Vakovian media before the sun goes down. It's probably on Twitter already."

Fitzsimmons sighed and turned, pacing back to his desk. He genuinely seemed more tired than angry. The ghost at the window had yet to even look at the others in the room.

"I don't know what to do," the major said finally. He turned back again, next to his desk, and shrugged. "What would you do?"

"Let me go," Shane answered.

"Now you're being... whatever it is you are. You've killed enough of my men these past few weeks for me to know you're not the kind of man who leaves a job unfinished. If our roles were reversed, you'd kill me."

"Our roles would never be reversed, so it's a faulty premise. I wouldn't murder civilians for money to help someone I've never heard of keep control of a country I don't care about," Shane said.

"Please don't bore me, Ryan. I just wanted to make money. I wanted to retire, and this mess keeps getting messier. You're right that no one cares about this country. You've never read about Vakovia in the news back home. You never saw a movie about the splendor of the Vakovian countryside. But now, because of you, this place is international news. And that's costly."

The man really seemed like an accountant. The dollars and cents of death were his chief concern.

"I wanted you dead. It would have been a lot easier if you were dead. In fact, I'd be back at my hotel packing my suitcase right now. I'd be scheduling my flight home, maybe booking dinner at my favorite restaurant. But I'm not."

Shane shrugged.

"Sorry to disappoint," he said.

"President Janosik wants you. Those are standing orders, and since we can't pretend you died in the field anymore, that's what's going to happen."

"Is he going to tell me what the border fence I destroyed cost?" Shane asked. Nothing he said caused Fitzsimmons' expression to change at all, and it was unnerving.

"Janosik is going to have you arrested, tried, convicted, and executed. So, you can look forward to a long, drawn-out process of pain. You will be tortured, I can almost guarantee that, and you will be branded a terrorist and a traitor and likely disowned by the Marines, the U.S. government, and anything else you've ever been affiliated with. No one will come to save you. The state department and the military have long since washed their hands of this because you have no idea who you're dealing with."

The ghost at the window finally glanced their way long enough to look Shane up and down. He was an unremarkable-looking fellow, beyond the hole someone had blown through his chest.

"That's a trite line, don't you think? 'You have no idea who you're dealing with'? That's movie-villain stuff," Shane said.

"It's a fact, Ryan. Nothing you've done will cause any long-term harm to Silvershore. We'll leave when you're dead, we'll regroup, and we'll go on another mission. Then another. Then another. Even Vakovia will forget us because the twin terrorists of Colonel Copland and Shane Ryan will have both died."

The two men stared at one another for a moment in silence. Shane waited for Fitzsimmons to continue, but he seemed to be waiting for Shane's reply.

"Am I supposed to react to that?" Shane asked. Finally, for a brief moment, the other man looked flustered, if only mildly.

"Doesn't matter. You're a dead man."

"So you've said," Shane replied. "But if you wanted me dead before, this is someone else's idea, isn't it? You're just a middleman? That's what's got you all anxious to pack up and leave town? Sick of doing someone else's work for them?"

The ghost at the window grunted.

"He's trying to push your buttons," the spirit said. His voice was as flat and forgettable as his face. That was, for many, a strength, however. It was always better to be forgettable than memorable when your job was killing.

"I don't have buttons," Fitzsimmons pointed out.

"Then you can tell me who runs the Reapers without feeling bad about it," Shane replied. The ghost grunted again.

"You're still planning to get out of this, aren't you?" Fitzsimmons said. He didn't smile, but there was a hint of enjoyment in his voice. "That's admirable in an odd way. You think you'll escape and hunt down the head of the dragon?"

"Something like that," Shane agreed.

"What do you think, Cuddy?" the major asked, looking at his spectral asset. The ghost at the window shrugged.

"I don't care."

"Neither do I," Fitzsimmons said.

He locked eyes with Shane, considering whether to continue.

"You know Copland wasn't running this outfit, and obviously, I'm not, either. You know Silvershore was the business front, the more sanitary and palatable face of what everyone else calls Reaper Company. You know we're running ops in Europe, at the very least, using spectral assets to ensure mission success. So, you're thinking… something big. Bigger, anyway."

The major's eyes narrowed as if trying to read something on Shane's face.

"Big enough to waste a ninety-million-dollar helicopter or two," Shane said.

"Yeah. Who's big enough to waste that kind of money in a podunk country like Vakovia?"

Shane gave the other man a considering look.

"You're saying Reaper Company is government-sanctioned? The U.S. military is behind this?"

"I didn't say anything, Ryan. Because you're going to die, and I've wasted weeks in this country spinning my wheels. Take him to the tombs."

Banner pulled on Shane's arm, dragging him back toward the door. Shane struggled in the man's grip, still zip-tied behind his back but unwilling to leave so soon.

"This is no sanctioned project. Who's running it?" Shane asked.

Fitzsimmons took his seat at the desk again while Banner pulled Shane away.

"Make sure he has a nice room," the major added.

"If you're so confident I'm going to die, why not tell me who's running the show, Fitzsimmons?" Shane asked.

What the major was saying did not check all the boxes. If the Reapers were government-sanctioned, why was anyone accepting money from people like Janosik? The government didn't need pocket change from tin-pot dictators. They wasted more on the helicopter than Janosik could have afforded to pay the Reapers for the job they were doing. It didn't make sense.

Politically, the U.S. gained nothing from Janosik being in charge of a country that had little to no presence on the world stage. The only way the Reapers made sense was if they were what they appeared to be, a mercenary company.

"Why not tell you?" Fitzsimmons said. He looked at the ghost standing at the window. "Cuddy, why don't I tell him?"

"Because he wants to know," the ghost answered.

"See you in another life, Ryan," the major added.

Banner yanked him again, harder this time, nearly knocking him over as he turned him around and pushed him out the door.

"Tell me you're not buying that," Shane said to the man with the gun in his back as they went back down the hall he'd just traveled to get to Fitzsimmons. Banner was joined by the entire Reaper team once more, along with their spectral assets, escorting Shane to the stairwell.

"You think this is official, Banner? You're all working for the military? You believe that?"

Banner didn't say anything, he just kept the gun in Shane's back. Shane couldn't piece it together. A rogue outfit with the military could operate overseas like the Reapers, maybe. But resource allocation would have been a nightmare for something trying to skim profit while still being sanctioned by the military. Fitzsimmons' focus on money made everything he said after contradictory.

If Shane had destroyed one hundred million in assets like he said, how could that be swept under the rug? How could a job that another normal mercenary company would have done for less than ten million be worth it?

Chapter 22
Paid in Blood

Banner and his men took Shane to the basement and then a sub-basement, deep under the building into what looked like a bomb shelter built sometime in the sixties.

The walls were made of concrete and steel, and they absorbed sound. Even footsteps fell flat as the group traveled the halls to a series of cells built into a stone sarcophagus of a room. No windows, no airflow, and no noise at all. Just concrete cells with steel bars sealing them in.

There were six cells in the room, all unoccupied. The interior of each held nothing. No bed, no sink, no toilet. Just concrete. Shane was thrown into one. and the door was locked after him.

"Any plans to cut these things off?" Shane asked, getting to his feet, and turning to show his zip-tied hands to Banner. The captain stood on the other side of the bars and shook his head.

"Don't see the point."

"I need to piss," Shane said dryly. Banner grinned.

"I'm not stopping you, soldier."

Banner left, taking the rest of the Reapers with him. The exterior entrance to the prison cell block, a massive steel blast door, was sealed, and a heavy-sounding lock rolled into place with a thud. Shane was alone.

He paced the small six-by-eight cell, looking for any variation in the concrete, but there was nothing. It was smooth and flat and devoid of even slight dips or depressions.

Shane turned his back to the bars and pressed the zip tie against one of the flat steel cross pieces that linked the bars in the cell door. He began rubbing the zip tie against it, slowly wearing it down. The metal was smooth, and little friction was created, but it was better than nothing. Ten minutes faded to twenty and then finally thirty. He strained and pulled his wrists while he rubbed until the plastic snapped.

Hands free, Shane was able to inspect the edges of the bars where they were set into the stone. He could find no weakness, no spot where the steel or the concrete was loose or susceptible to manipulation.

The overhead lights, sealed behind plastic embedded in the ceiling, flickered. Shane moved from bar to bar, tracing the base of each with his finger. He tried the hinges in the door, and the locking mechanism. Nothing seemed damaged or out of place.

Across the hall, the empty cell facing Shane went dark. The light in the hall buzzed and dimmed.

"Hello?" Shane said.

He had not seen any of the spectral assets come back into the room, but he was confident a ghost had made its way back to him. If it was one of the Reapers, he wondered what they'd come back for. Janosik wanted to execute him, so they couldn't kill him just yet.

Lights flickered in the hall and then went dead. All lights save Shane's went out. He stood under the concealed bulb looking out at blackness, the world around him no longer visible.

Shane stepped back from the bars and waited. The hallway light flickered on and off again, showing the empty concrete path between cells in quick, strobing glimpses of shadow and bare stone.

"You're really wasting the effort," Shane said. The lights continued to flicker. Off for a minute, flashing for seconds, off again. He waited for the ghost he knew was out there to make a move.

The light buzzed on, and Shane was caught by surprise. He could see a spirit fading in and out of his field of view in the constantly flickering light. Smeared with blood, puffy and purple with rigor mortis, the face looking back at him belonged to Davis Blakely.

Blakely smiled. Viscous, dark blood drizzled between his teeth and flowed like molasses down his chin. Shane stayed still.

"You look like hell, Blakely," he said.

The lights went dark again, save for the one in Shane's cell. He waited as that, too, began to flicker. It went dark and Shane was plunged into blackness. He stayed still, feeling the air around him grow colder.

The light flickered once more, and Blakely was in the cell, face to face with him. Shane was thrust back against the rear wall. He slammed into the concrete and fell to the floor. Blakely was on top of him in a second. The light strobed, and the ghost's foot slammed into his gut like a sledgehammer.

Shane grunted, and another kick took him between the shoulder blades. A second ghost had entered the cell, one he hadn't seen, and the two continued kicking as a third slammed a foot into the small of his back from the underside.

He reached out to grab Blakely's ankle, and a foot slammed down on his wrist. Blakely crouched, only it was not Blakely's face anymore. The illusion wavered so close, and Shane could see a different face, one of the spectral assets from St. Jude's, smiling grimly.

"I heard you were tough," the ghost said.

He slammed a fist into Shane's jaw as the other two continued kicking him in the shoulders, head, back, and gut.

Shane spit blood at the ghost and smiled back.

"Of the two of us, I'm the only one who's still alive," he said. The ghost's expression grew darker.

"For now," he agreed, his purple face inches from Shane's. "But you'll wish you weren't."

The purple spirit looked at the other two ghosts, and they stopped their assault. Frozen hands grabbed Shane's bruised body and forced him to his knees while his hands were pulled behind his back. Another set of hands grasped his neck and forced his head up.

The ghost that had appeared as Blakely pushed its fingers into Shane's mouth. They were cold and thick and probed between his lips and past his tongue. Shane tried to bite, but the ghost holding his neck held onto his jaw as well, forcing his mouth open.

Shane stared into the ghost's eyes as he felt the spirit take hold of one of his premolars. Cold, dead fingers squeezed the tooth and pulled it hard to the right, toward Shane's cheek. He felt the pressure build and heard a crunching inside of his skull. The ghosts held him firmly, preventing any struggle as his jaw resisted until it was no longer able.

The root of the tooth came loose with a crunchy pop, and blood flooded Shane's mouth. The ghost pulled the tooth out and held it in front of Shane's face, still red with blood and some small bits of tissue attached to the root.

"This goes in my collection," the spirit said.

He pushed Shane back against the wall and kicked him in the face. Shane's head bounced off of the concrete, and his vision swam. The remaining blows felt like nothing to him as his body went numb and he blacked out.

***

Shane awoke to another kick in his gut. The purple ghost had returned.

"Wake up, cutie. We're not done yet," the ghost said.

Shane wanted to reply with something witty despite the pain that throbbed across his body. He felt like one big, angry bruise from head to toe.

The cell was freezing cold, whether from the ghosts or an intentional temperature shift, he didn't know. Anything he planned to say was muffled as the ghost's thick, frosty hand was forced to the back of his throat once more. The ghost hummed as he worked, grabbing hold of another of

Shane's teeth and pulling on it harshly.

Bone crunched, and blood flowed once more until the tooth broke free. Satisfied with his work, the ghost again held it up for Shane to see.

"How many more do you think I can take before you need to leave?"

The ghost grinned an expression of almost childlike glee. He looked around and then leaned in, his bloated, purple cheek against Shane's.

"You'll never guess what I start taking when you run out of teeth," he whispered into Shane's ear.

Cold hands closed around his throat. He wanted to break free but was too weak. The ghost squeezed, not trying to break his neck, not even trying to kill him, just enough to slow the flow of blood and oxygen. Without the ability to defend himself, Shane was at the ghost's mercy and soon found his eyes rolling back in his head as he lost consciousness again.

✳ ✳ ✳

Shane awoke to a sense of movement. His eyes fluttered open and struggled to focus. The lights were on again, and they were passing over his head. He heard a scraping sound and realized it was his body being dragged. Someone was pulling him by the legs.

He lifted his head, and pain throbbed through his skull and neck and back. His mouth felt swollen, and he remembered the ghost taking out his teeth.

Two Reapers dragged him by the legs out of the prison cell and down the hall through the basement. Others walked alongside, their guns trained on him. His hands had been zip-tied together, this time in front of his body.

"Checkout time already?" he muttered, pronouncing the words awkwardly with his puffy mouth.

"This guy never stops with the jokes," one of the Reapers said.

"Just doing a stand-up tour of Vakovia," Shane added.

He was too sore to struggle against them as they pulled him down the hall.

"Can you walk, Ryan?" Banner asked.

The procession through the basement stopped and Shane's feet were dropped. The Green Beret captain appeared over him, looking down at him.

"Sure, let's give it a try," he said.

The Reapers waited as he rolled awkwardly onto his side, holding in groans of pain as he used his shackled hands to support himself as he got to his knees.

"Pull him up," Banner said.

A hand under each armpit hoisted him. Shane was shaky, but he stayed upright. In front of him, with a trio of Reapers, the purple ghost took a step forward.

"Smile, big guy. Let's see those pearly whites," the ghost said.

Shane smiled and lifted his shackled hands quickly, hooking them over the purple ghost's neck as he pulled both of them against the wall. A half-dozen guns raised and aimed at his head, while Shane held the ghost's neck beneath his bound wrists. Only Banner's gun remained down.

"Ryan, what the hell are you doing?" the captain asked.

"Going for a walk with you fine fellows," Shane answered. "Why? Want to do something else?"

"If you think you can take a hostage—"

Shane pulled back as hard as he could, ignoring Banner and twisting the purple ghost's head sharply. There was an audible sound of breaking and Shane lifted a foot, kicking out the ghost's knee as he continued to pull up. The ghost's head snapped from his body and Shane spun away, using his bruised back to shield himself from the explosion of energy as best as he could.

The spirits and the men were forced back as the percussive wave hit everyone like a fist. Guns were back up and aimed in seconds, but Shane had not tried to escape. He didn't think he could run if he wanted to.

"Hostage? Why would I take a hostage?" Shane asked.

"Jesus," one of the Reapers muttered as Banner finally pulled his own sidearm.

"About face and march, soldier. One way or another, you are dying today," the Green Beret ordered.

Shane held up his hands defensively and turned, limping toward the Reapers, who had yet to move. A glance at Banner and they started again, two men turning their back on Shane and the rest falling behind with their guns level and ready to fire.

"You ever seen anything like that?" the Reaper behind Shane whispered to the men with him.

"Shut up and do your job," Banner said, cutting off anyone's answer. He was as angry as Shane had seen him. That helped take some of the sting from his wounds.

CHAPTER 23
THE GREAT ESCAPE

The journey up the stairs was taking too long for Banner's liking. Shane's legs were knotted with bruises, and he might have opted to overplay his injuries just for the hell of it. After awkwardly scaling five steps, Reapers dragged him the rest of the way to the ground floor of the building.

Banner led the way to the SUV convoy, parked out front where they'd left it when Shane was dropped off. Fitzsimmons and Cuddy were already on the street, and they got into the lead SUV as Shane and the others appeared.

"You have no idea how glad I am to be done with you, Ryan," Banner said, forcing him into the back of the second-to-last vehicle in the convoy. "I gotta say, though. In another life, I bet it would have been a wild ride to serve with you."

"Doubt it," Shane said, settling into his seat. "I never liked serving with assholes."

Banner smiled and took the seat next to Shane in the rear of the vehicle.

"I'm going to have a drink to celebrate your execution."

"Maybe I'll do the same," Shane said.

Banner chuckled and pounded a fist on the ceiling of the vehicle.

"Let's get this the hell over with," he said.

The engine roared to life, and their driver got in line, following the other SUVs away from the dull office building that was the Reapers' temporary home.

Shane watched the streets of Ravjek pass as the convoy weaved through old neighborhoods to whatever building Shane's trial was set to take place in. After two blocks, he noticed something had changed in the city since his last visit several weeks earlier. There wasn't a single ghost to be seen.

If any of the Reapers were aware that things had changed on Ravjek's streets, they gave no sign. The city had been home to an abundance of the dead before, like all places in Vakovia, but as they traveled, he couldn't see a single one, even in windows or alleys.

The SUVs were traveling through one of the oldest parts of the city. The concentration of spirits had always been dense there when Shane was in town.

Another block, and Shane noticed that the living were also now missing from the streets. There was no one around anywhere.

The convoy approached an intersection, and the first several vehicles passed through the green light. Shane looked over at Banner, glancing past the man to the window and the view of the street they were passing in time to see the front end of a square, white delivery truck plow through the red light.

The truck clipped the back end of the SUV and spun it through the intersection. Shane held on as the truck crashed into the front of a restaurant, coming to a rest in the dining area.

"Go now! Secure Ryan!" Banner shouted, holding his hand to a gash across his forehead caused by the shattered window. He turned to look at their prisoner, half his face covered in blood. "Whatever this is, it won't work."

A series of loud noises popped out on the street, and something hot and moist hit Shane. Blood, he realized A bullet passed through Banner's head and embedded in the frame of the SUV. The soldier's blood misted across the back seat and left his face a mask of red.

The driver of the SUV slumped over the wheel. The Reaper on the front passenger seat had escaped the vehicle but he was taken out by another bullet, and Shane was unable to even see where the shooter was positioned.

Three spectral assets were guarding Shane from the outside. He craned his neck and watched a trio of armed men across the street taking shots at the other SUVs.

A ghost crept through the restaurant on Shane's other side. He caught the movement from his peripheral vision and turned to see that it was not alone. A dozen ghosts slinked through the shadows. Some glanced at him but said nothing. They were not coming for him.

The restaurant ghosts swarmed over the SUV, climbing under, over, and through to attack the three spectral assets. Shane moved as soon as they engaged. He pulled a knife from Banner's belt and used it to cut his bonds, and then rifled through the man's pockets until he found his lighter and the small box where they placed Radek's haunted item.

Shane pulled the icy-cold pin from the box and slipped it into his pocket as he fled the SUV into the half-destroyed restaurant.

"Looks like things have escalated," Radek said, appearing at Shane's side. He nodded to the ghost, running for the far side of the restaurant and out onto the cross street.

"We're in Ravjek. Someone just broke me out, I think," Shane told the ghost.

"Who?"

"No idea," Shane answered. His list of Vakovian allies was short, especially those who could mount an offensive against the Reapers.

The streets echoed with automatic gunfire. Dozens of ghosts swarmed the firefight, and none of them were spectral assets. The dead of Ravjek as well as some of the living had come together, and they were laying waste to the Reapers.

Shane ran from the firefight with Radek at his side, confused but not one to argue in the middle of a war zone. Shane didn't know who saved him, but he wouldn't risk being shot to find out.

"We have to get to the front of that chain of SUVs," Shane said, pausing at the rear of the restaurant to look down the narrow alley.

Ravjek was full of old alleys that used to be where residents slopped their sewage out of a window with a bucket. Now, they were latticework connecting the streets behind buildings and places where rats and the dead hid from the sun.

Shane darted down the alley to the next block, ignoring the aches in his muscles and bones, and then crept back up to the street. The gunfire had escalated to what sounded like all-out war.

At the corner, an unlabeled delivery truck was parked askew, and three men used it as cover to fire at an unknown target. Even from behind, Shane could tell they weren't Reapers, they were whoever had forced the convoy off the road.

The shooter at the front of the truck ducked behind the tire to avoid a flurry of gunshots. The man made eye contact with Shane, a smile spreading across his broad face.

"American!" Vanko shouted.

The Russian gangster had been an invaluable asset to Shane before he left Ravjek, providing him with supplies and vehicles. Shane ran to the truck, keeping low to stay out of sight of the Reapers.

"This was you?" Shane said, approaching the man. The Russian clapped him on the shoulder.

"I came to rescue you! But you are here, so what the hell am I shooting at?"

"No idea," Shane replied. "Couldn't hurt to take a few more of those guys out, though."

"*Raketa!*" one of Vanko's men shouted in Russian.

"I know that word," Radek said, and Shane nodded. It was Russian for rocket.

Vanko and Shane ran from the truck, back toward the alley, moments before a rocket-propelled grenade hit the Russian's truck, exploding the front end.

Within seconds, tires were squealing on the road and one of the SUVs was moving again. It had to be Fitzsimmons. He was going to get away. If he did, so would any chance Shane had of finding out who gave out the orders for Reaper Company.

"We need that SUV," Shane said, turning on his heels, and running back to the road.

"But I just rescued you from SUVs," Vanko protested.

The Russian groaned and gave chase, following Shane to the firefight, which had been greatly diminished since the truck blew up and Fitzsimmons escaped.

The road was littered with bodies, most of them Reapers but a good number of men who looked like civilians as well. Shane ran to the first of the abandoned SUVs and found a dead Reaper at the wheel, a handful of bullet wounds peppered across his body. He pulled the corpse from the vehicle and got in.

"I appreciate the rescue, but I need to get to the man in charge before he finds a helicopter and flees," Shane said out the window as Vanko caught up. With a turn of the key, the engine roared to life.

"Wait wait wait!" Vanko protested, slamming his hands on the hood as he circled the front end. Gunshots rang out, and he flinched and hustled, pulling open the passenger door as Radek hopped in the back.

"I spend all this time plotting amazing escape, and you rush back to your captor? I'm coming with you," Vanko insisted.

Shane was about to protest when the rear windows were shot out. He put the vehicle in gear, hit the gas, and headed after Fitzsimmons.

The streets of Ravjek had emptied, and Shane was met with a clear path. They were taking him to Janosik in the courthouse in the center of the city. It was Ravjek's oldest building, and the most secure. Fitzsimmons could find reinforcements there, either police or military.

Shane had spent time walking Ravjek's streets before he took on the

Reapers, getting to know the lay of the land. He wanted to make sure he'd never be caught in unfamiliar territory and had plenty of ways to make the most of the landscape. Fitzsimmons had only just arrived in town, and Shane doubted he'd spent a lot of time getting to know the place.

The SUV lurched as Shane took a sharp left. He sped down side streets, easy to navigate thanks to Vanko's work clearing civilians to avoid casualties. Narrow passageways that were often hard to navigate in traffic were clear, and they sped by until Shane reached the city's massive outdoor market.

Far enough from the firefight, the market was still teeming with people, though decidedly fewer than Shane was used to. The vast bazaar cut off a large portion of the downtown area and forced traffic to go wide to avoid it, especially on the main road that Fitzsimmons had probably taken.

Shane skirted the edge of the market and then cut across in time to see a black SUV.

"You're going to want to put your seatbelt on," Shane told Vanko.

The gangster cursed in Russian and pulled the belt tight as Shane hit the gas and angled his SUV toward the fleeing vehicle, the side of it pockmarked with bullet holes from Vanko's assault.

The windows were tinted, and Shane couldn't get a clear look at Fitzsimmons to know if he even saw Shane coming at him perpendicular to the road that bordered the market. Part of him hoped it was a surprise, there would have been some satisfaction in the man realizing what was happening at the last second.

Shane lurched forward in his seat and the airbag caught his head. Pain radiated throughout his body as the SUV clipped the rear of Fitzsimmons' vehicle and sent them both spinning into nearby buildings.

Shane and the others came to a rest against the wall of a coffeehouse. He pushed the deflated airbag out of his way and reached over for Vanko.

"You good?" he asked.

"Good? No. You tried to kill us," he replied. "But I did survive."

"Good," Shane said. He forced his now bent door open and stumbled out onto the road.

The other SUV had crashed through the entrance to the coffee shop, and only the rear of the vehicle was visible. Shane approached slowly, looking for signs of movement, when Radek surprised him from behind, resting a hand on his shoulder.

"There," the ghost said, pointing to the market. On the far side, past a table set up with bushels of fruit, Fitzsimmons and Cuddy were heading toward a side street.

The major looked back and locked eyes with Shane. When they had first met, Fitzsimmons had been blasé and disinterested. He betrayed almost no emotion. But when their eyes locked across the market, Shane saw something there. Fear.

Chapter 24
LAST STAND

"They will kill you," Vanko said, joining him on the street outside of the market. Shane looked at the man, unsure of what he meant, and the Russian pointed over the tops of the nearby buildings to the spire on top of the courthouse, visible from where they stood.

"This is why I came to save you. Janosik has the military on hand for your execution. Security to keep your so-called terrorist friends at bay."

"You're being executed today?" Radek asked.

Shane shook his head. He didn't have time to worry about what a man he never met was planning. Fitzsimmons was already gone and getting farther away by the second.

"That man's the only person who has the answers I need. I have to find him," Shane said. Vanko grunted and pulled a phone from his pocket.

"Then try to torture him for at least thirty minutes. I need time to organize," he said.

"You a freedom fighter now, Vanko?"

"Maybe," he said. "Or maybe I'm getting official pardon from Peter Zemba if he takes power. Who's to say? Go find your man."

Shane left him by the crashed SUVs and ran across the market. The city was still alive with the sound of distant gunshots and sirens, but none had come close to the market. Time was running out for Shane, but he had learned the roads all around the market as a precaution.

Radek followed him as he cut through alleys and through a bakery where the owner was hiding behind his display case. If Fitzsimmons was heading to the courthouse, there were only so many ways he could travel to get there.

"That man said you were to be executed," Radek pointed out as they ran.

Shane nodded. Every step sent shocks of pain up his legs, through his spine, and all across his body. The bruises felt raw and exposed, but he could not stop.

"I was told there'd be a trial," Shane said. Radek laughed.

"I missed a lot when I was in that box," the ghost said. "And we are running toward the site of your execution?"

"Looks like," Shane agreed, taking a right down another alley. They were approaching another main road, close to the courthouse. The sound of his footfalls echoed off the walls, louder now than the distant gunshots as the remaining Reapers fought Vanko's forces.

Shane slowed when they reached the next street. Though there was no traffic here, not even pedestrians, they were not alone. A single figure waited for him in the shadows of a small, rundown apartment building. A ghost dressed in a green uniform. Fitzsimmons' spectral asset, Cuddy.

"You know this one?" Radek asked.

"Continental Marine," Shane answered. "Belongs to the one I'm after."

Cuddy was as unimpressive in the street as he had been in Fitzsimmons' office. The hole in his chest was smaller from the front, showing only the smallest glimpse of what lay behind him. He was pale, but not in the way many ghosts were, just in the way people who don't go outside a lot look pale. His face was puffy, and his hair was disheveled and poorly cut.

"Fitzsimmons left you as a distraction?" Shane asked. The ghost offered a half-shrug.

"His plan was that I'd kill you."

"And your plan?" Shane asked.

"Kill you."

Shane grunted, unsure of what other answer he expected. He approached the ghost quickly, and Cuddy waited for him. When he was within range, the dead Marine threw a low punch, causing Shane to stop and block.

Cuddy fought like a boxer, moving, and throwing punches in quick succession. He worked Shane's body then threw a surprise cross to his face before hitting another jab toward his gut. Shane was forced back, using his arms to avoid painful blows and deflect where he could.

Few ghosts fought the living with the expectation that they would be able to defend or fight back, but that was what Cuddy was doing. It kept Shane on the defensive and forced him to contend with the ghost rather than dispatching him quickly, as had been Shane's initial plan.

"I don't mean to interrupt, but if you need a hand…" Radek offered, watching from the side.

"I'm not trying to win honor points here," Shane said.

The paratrooper responded by rushing Cuddy and tackling him around the waist. Both ghosts fell through the wall of the apartment building and Shane left them there, following the path where Fitzsimmons had gone.

Shane ran down the nearest alley to the next street over. He was three blocks from the courthouse but had not seen Fitzsimmons again. He ran faster, making a beeline for the building in the hopes of catching up with the major before he got in sight of whatever security the President had called in. Even with Radek and Vanko as backups, if Janosik had surrounded the building with the Vakovian military, Shane would have no chance of catching Fitzsimmons.

Shane's legs were swept out from under him just as he reached the street. Cuddy fell on him, part of his uniform missing and his jaw misaligned. The ghost punched Shane in the ribs, right below his armpit, and then knelt on his stomach.

"You've lost the battle," Cuddy said, his speech muddled by his broken jaw. Shane punched him in the chin, exacerbating the break, and Radek tackled him once more.

"He's slippery," the paratrooper said, pummeling the other ghost as Shane scrambled back to his feet. "Go!"

Shane left them behind once more, the sound of breaking bone and tearing flesh filling his ears as Radek pushed Cuddy's jaw away from the rest of his skull. The ghost neither screamed nor cried out.

Shane cut through a hookah shop and went out the back door into a new alley. His chest was already growing tight, and breathing was becoming harder, but he pushed on. His injuries were slowing him, but he could not let Fitzsimmons get away. He was his only chance at finding out who was behind all this.

He had come farther than any of his previous scouting missions had taken him. He'd never approached the courthouse before, having no desire to get that close to the law in Ravjek. He was as blind now as Fitzsimmons would have been.

Part of his brain told him he was running in the wrong direction. The President planned to execute him, and Shane was heading right toward where they planned to do it. Vanko had freed him, gifted him his life. He should have been fleeing. The Reapers were crippled, maybe disabled entirely now. It was his best chance to leave the country and find a way back home. But he couldn't do it. He needed to put an end to Reaper Company, and that meant discovering who was at the top of the heap.

Someone stateside was calling the shots for Copland and Fitzsimmons. Someone was creating an army of men and ghosts that would be sold to the highest bidder, and Shane had become a piece on a gameboard to sell the idea. He didn't like that, and he wasn't going to allow it.

Shane had reached the street on which the courthouse waited. A massive courtyard in front of the building featured a statue of a battle scene with men on horseback, and a large fountain with benches was situated around it.

The structure rose high above the courtyard, accessible up a wide flight of stone steps. Pillars supported the roof over the building's entrance, a massive pair of green copper doors flanked by a dozen smaller wooden ones to either side. The exterior was carved with gargoyles and angels and horses and animals, all the way up to the enormous green copper dome that was set in the middle of a large, flat platform, visible from nearly everywhere in the city.

The people were gone, scared away by the gunfire or something else entirely. Jeeps were parked out front of the courthouse, forming a kind of barrier behind a separate one made of steel fencing. But none of that caught Shane's attention like the dead.

Ghosts had not fled the courthouse. The courtyard was home to scattered handfuls, but the courthouse was swarming with them. Hundreds of spirits loitered around the steps and walls.

Shane had yet to enter the courtyard, and he held back, not wanting to be spotted by Janosik's forces. Even at a distance, he could see the ghosts at the courthouse were not the same as the dead that were scattered across Vakovia. These were not the peaceful spirits of farmers or victims of ancient wars. These were something different.

Many of the dead were missing hands. Others were held in shackles. They were shirtless, and Shane could see that many bore identical scars across their backs, signs of whipping and torture. The courthouse dead were victims of Vakovian justice both ancient and recent. The convicted, tried, and executed who had died there, punished for their crimes.

Many of the oldest spirits, dressed in rags or not at all, were caked in filth and had died on the brink of starvation. They appeared as walking skeletons with the barest hints of flesh on their bruised and battered bodies.

Other ghosts showed signs of more creative and cruel tortures. The handless were most obvious, probably convicted thieves. Others had been stripped of flesh down their backs.

Puffy, purple scars lined many a neck, the victims of hangings. Others were riddled with gunshot wounds, clustered together in the chest and gut, the victims of firing squads.

Shane wondered how many people went to work every day in the old courthouse and had no idea how many of the dead watched them go up those stairs. How many people worked and ate lunch and got paid on what must have been a dragon's hoard worth of bones and haunted items somewhere below their feet.

"You cannot go in the front," a voice said in Hungarian. The ghost of a boy with a missing leg leaned on the alley wall across from Shane. "They usually leave the living alone, but if they know you can see them, they will not be happy."

"They attack people?" Shane asked. The boy nodded.

"Not out here. But they will follow you inside. Get you alone somewhere. People fall out windows on the upper floors too often. Or they're found hanging in restrooms. These dead don't like to be seen."

"Ghosts that don't like to be seen usually hide."

The boy shook his head and pointed at something Shane could not make out.

"They cannot hide because what's in the dark is worse," he whispered.

"What's in the dark?" Shane asked.

The boy sighed and looked away.

"The bad ones."

"The angry ones," a voice corrected.

The ghost of a man joined the boy. He was much older, with gray hair and a heavily lined face. He wore a small red fez and blood leaked from under the rim.

"You were chasing that man," the elderly ghost said.

He nodded to the courthouse, and Shane looked. A figure was climbing the steps to the front door. It was hard to see any clear features at a distance, but he didn't need to. He recognized the uniform well enough. It was Fitzsimmons. He had made it to his sanctuary. There was an entire courtyard, and an army of ghosts Shane could not easily sneak past without giving himself away. He'd escaped.

Shane cursed. Janosik would learn Shane was free and deploy the military. He'd be forced underground again. He'd be back to where he started after Copland's death, trying to escape the country while they hunted him.

"I have to get in there," he said, turning to the elderly ghost.

"There is no safe way in," the old man answered.

"I didn't say safely," Shane replied. "I just need a way that no one will see. Is there anything?"

"There is a way. But even those ghosts will not take it."

"Tell me," Shane said.

Chapter 25
WHAT WAITS BELOW

The elderly ghost led Shane around the courtyard, behind buildings, and out of sight of both the living and the dead. They were adjacent to the courthouse when the ghost stopped on an old cobblestone street in front of a sewer covering. Shane sighed.

"Of course," he muttered. He had already spent far too much time in Vakovian sewers. Enough time to know how rancid the sewers of Ravjek were.

"There was a dungeon below the courthouse," the ghost said, ignoring Shane's distaste for the path he had to follow. "The government sealed it off more than half a century ago to bring Vakovia into a new age and ignore the horrors of the past. They sealed it up as though it never was. But it is still there."

"The dungeon is where the angry ghosts stay?" Shane asked. The elderly spirit nodded.

"They could leave. They could come into the sun as the rest of us do, even as that mob before the courthouse does. But they are no longer beings of light. They are Vakovia's greatest atrocities. Men and women driven beyond madness by pain and torment. Their humanity was stripped from them just as their flesh was. Their spirits returned as creatures of despair. They are manifestations of anguish and rage. It is unsafe for anyone, anything, to venture down there. But if the man who defeated the demon cannot succeed, then I do not know who could."

Shane grunted. The whisper network was alive and well. They knew he had fought their demon near Hannec. But the dead in the dungeon would probably not care.

"We have another demon to kill?" Radek asked.

The ghost approached slowly, and Shane could see he was no longer in peak condition. Cuddy had damaged him badly. His left hand was gone, and pieces of his body had been torn away as if gnawed off by animals.

"You don't have to come with me this time," Shane said. The paratrooper looked offended.

"It is you who need not come with me, Ryan. Radek Dorn's revenge is only beginning. I will drag this Janosik into the ground kicking and screaming if I need to."

"Revenge?"

"For Oleg," his companion said. "He was my friend. You are my friend. The only I have had in a lifetime and more. I do not give up on my friends. Do you?"

"No," Shane said. "Then we should go before Fitzsimmons slips away to a place where I can't find him."

Shane pried the cover off the sewer entrance and scowled as the rank smell washed over him. Ravjek was not under the same heatwave it was when he had been in the sewer before, but it was still hot, and things had not improved. The air was humid and thick, and the stench was stomach-turning. He envied Radek for not being able to smell it.

He dropped down into ankle-deep filth and felt the warm liquid soak his shoes. Radek followed soon after, and they made their way down the pipe in the direction of the courthouse.

The elderly ghost had told Shane there were numerous entrances into the dungeon. The dungeon had been sealed from the courthouse side, but no one cared about sealing it from below. No one would break into such a place, they assumed. It was not as though the courthouse was a bank vault.

Shane trudged through the filth using his lighter and Radek's keener vision to guide them. The tunnel extended under what Shane assumed was the length of the courtyard and branched left, around where he suspected the courthouse might be.

They followed the path as it turned left, and the level of muck diminished until he was eventually in a dry passageway. Another branch gave the option of straight ahead or to the right, and Shane chose right.

"This has to be under the courthouse, right?" he asked.

"I could check," Radek offered. Shane shook his head. With all the angry-looking spirits above them, it was too much of a risk for Radek to pop up out of nowhere. It might give Shane's position away.

The elderly ghost had been right about the courtyard ghosts. None of them were underground. No spirits wandered the sewers at all, not even the dangerous ones Shane had been warned about. He wondered what was keeping them at bay as he and Radek followed a much narrower tunnel under the building.

"There," Radek said, pointing up.

Shane looked and saw a narrow passage straight up into darkness. An exceptionally thin ladder was set into the stone wall, barely wide enough for a man of Shane's size to fit across the shoulders.

"Tight squeeze," he said, holding the lighter higher to see what lay ahead. The edges of the light flickered and danced, but the darkness seemed impenetrable.

"What's up there?" he asked.

Radek stared into the darkness and then looked up again.

"I think we should take the ladder," he suggested.

Shane looked him in the eye, then looked back down the tunnel to the darkness.

"You see something?" he asked.

The ghost shook his head.

"That's the problem. I can't see anything back there. Nothing beyond the edge of your light. Nothing the way we came, either."

Shane turned and looked back. The flame cast a small circle of light, and then there was only inky blackness. The tunnel had been dark before, but something was different now, harder to explain.

"We go up," Shane agreed. He would have to extinguish the flame.

Radek waited below as Shane ascended the narrow ladder, barely able to go hand over hand in the tight space. Something began to hum down below, and it was not the ghost of the paratrooper.

Stone rubbed against Shane's elbows, and he winced, feeling flesh grate away as he moved as quickly as he could. He reached the top, and his hands fumbled blindly at a metal plate covering the exit. He felt around until his finger pressed into an indentation. Dirt and muck gave way, and he pushed through a hole.

The humming was growing louder. It wasn't a tune, just an unstructured and random sound that rose and lowered, almost like someone falling asleep trying to mumble words.

"Can you open it?" Radek asked.

Shane pushed up. He had very little leverage to work with in the small space, and it was hard, but the panel above his head began to give.

"It's moving," he said.

"Good," came Radek's reply. He was not in the tunnel any longer but directly above Shane on the other side of the panel.

The metal scraped, and the ghost was able to give Shane the extra leverage he needed to pull it aside. Radek's good hand grabbed Shane's wrist, his grip cold and firm, and he pulled him from the ladder.

"Close it," the ghost instructed.

The hum was directly below them now, at the base of the ladder. Shane stared down into the darkness but still saw nothing. He took hold of the plate that covered the tunnel, pulled it half over, and then stopped himself.

He could not see Radek in the dark of wherever they were now, but he needed to. He retrieved the lighter from his pocket and struck it, bringing the flame to life. The ghost was standing over him, looking down the hole.

Shane looked down as well. The fire flickered and cast shadows that were swallowed by the solid darkness below it. The humming continued.

"What's down there?" Shane asked.

"I don't want to know. Do you?" he asked.

"No. I don't think so," Shane replied. He pulled the panel over the hole and resealed it. Some mysteries were best left unsolved, and he was on a clock.

The dungeon was what Shane expected it to be. With the lighter raised above his head, he could see crumbling stone walls and carved, arched doorways leading to additional chambers. There were cells set into the stone walls, closed and empty, each with ancient chains and manacles attached to the floor or walls.

The stone was stained in many places. The stains all looked like black splashes in the dim light of the lighter, but Shane had no doubt about what he saw.

Ghosts stood around them like a crowd of spectators. They had waited for him to climb out of the hole in the floor, and now, it seemed, they waited for something else.

Dozens of spirits stood frozen and silent. Each was a disfigured canvas of pain and cruelty. Many lacked parts, clearly dismembered in at least a partially surgical fashion. On many of the ghosts, hands, arms, legs, and feet had been severed by blades. Others had been peeled like grapes, their flesh pulled back to expose ribs, spines, and innards.

More than one spirit was burned. Some must have had hot pokers taken to their eyes, and others had been placed over fires, resulting in black feet like chunks of charcoal that didn't resemble flesh again until well above the blistered, weeping knees and thighs.

Every torture Shane could imagine—and some that he never would have—must have been conducted in the dungeons of Ravjek at some time. And the resulting spirits no longer even resembled anything human.

"We're just here to kill a man," Radek said in Chechen.

Someone laughed in the dark, a high-pitched and manic sound. The ghosts parted like grass being pushed aside by a rushing animal, and a dark, hunched form lunged at Shane, knocking him over.

The ghost was growling and grunting, and Shane had not had time to prepare himself before it attacked. On the ground, it went for his face. Cold, sharp teeth bit into his lip and cheek, and he yelled in pain as he struck the ghost in the face as hard as he could.

The blow surprised the thing, which he could barely see now. It reeled back, allowing Shane to sit up and hit it again in the mouth. In the flickering light of the fallen lighter, it looked like a broken and hunched-over man with no meat on his bones, many of which were broken and protruding through the thin, dark flesh of his emaciated frame.

The ghost laughed, the manic laugh of the insane, and Shane deflected another attack. He rolled the broken ghost over and knelt on its already shattered chest. It howled and cackled and leaned forward enough to bite Shane's thigh.

Shane twisted the ghost's head from his leg, pushing it to the dirty floor of the dungeon, and pressed down hard. The skull crushed and the ghost burst, sending a shockwave through the crowd of assembled watchers.

Murmurs rose, voices that grew in fear and anger, as the dead huddled closer.

"We should go now," Radek suggested.

"Good plan," Shane said.

He got to his feet and made his way through the nearest archway to a nearly identical room. Ghosts pressed near, but he pushed through them using shoulders and elbows to force them back.

The murmuring grew louder, and a few shouts rose above the rest. Hands grabbed at Shane, and he lashed out swiftly, punching jaws or elbowing ribs before moving on. Fighting was a bad option, and if they attacked as a group, neither he nor Radek stood a chance.

The next room led to stairs carved into the stone. Shane took the steps two by two to a locked door that opened onto wooden slats and clumped plaster. Someone had walled the door over and nothing more.

The ghosts of the dungeon clamored around the stairs but seemed hesitant to ascend. Shane put a foot through the frail wall and then used his shoulder to knock the rest of it out of his way. He stumbled out into a basement hall, empty of people but lit and much warmer than the dungeon. They were in the courthouse.

"Let's hope there's still time," Radek said, joining him in the hall.

Below, the ghosts of the dungeon stared up at the exit. None of them made a move toward it.

CHAPTER 26
The Fallen King

The courthouse rumbled. Even in the basement, Shane heard the thunder of feet down hallways and stairs. People were moving, fast and in large numbers. He could hear the odd thump and boom above the din. Something was happening, and it was chaotic.

Radek and Shane ran the length of a basement hall past storage rooms, archives, and other facilities that the courthouse either used very little or had already been evacuated because of whatever was happening upstairs.

When they reached the end of the hall and found an actual stairwell, the sound above was like thunder. Dozens of footfalls echoed as people ran down to the main floor.

Shane looked up from the basement, peering through the tiny space that existed in the middle of the curving stairwell. He could see arms, men in uniform, all heading down in the same direction. Dozens of men came down from the fourth and third floors, all in identical uniforms, all leaving the stairwell on the floor above the basement.

Something shook the walls, and dust fell in streams. Shane looked at Radek.

"Mortar fire?" the ghost suggested. It could have been. Some kind of explosion had taken place outside in the courtyard. The courthouse was under attack.

"Vanko," Shane said. The gangster must have regrouped with his men.

"All of your friends are destructive," Radek said with a grin. "It's very helpful."

The soldiers thundering down the stairs had filtered out to parts unknown, allowing Shane and Radek to head upstairs. He moved cautiously but quickly, listening for any stragglers before reaching the first-floor doors.

"Where is this man we're hunting going to be?" Radek asked.

The courthouse was big, and Fitzsimmons could have been anywhere. He would need to report to Janosik at some point, though, and it seemed like the President was distracted now, thanks to Vanko bombarding the building from outside. Fitzsimmons might be waiting his turn somewhere.

"Let's just look and see," Shane replied.

There had to be an office or something that the President worked from. He and Fitzsimmons could be hiding there. If they were not, then they were looking to escape, and that meant a back door. Unless it didn't.

Distant gunfire and men's shouts were already echoing through the courthouse walls, but a second sound was behind it, steady, and growing louder. A helicopter was inbound.

"We need to get to the roof," Shane suggested.

"It's a dome," Radek pointed out.

"Not all of it," Shane said.

He raced up the stairs with Radek, taking them two by two up to the second, third, and fourth floors. He was already winded, but the helicopter was much louder now. The thunder of the blades was unmistakable, even when he couldn't see it. It was the second King Stallion. The Reapers were fleeing. Fitzsimmons was getting away.

Two more floors and Shane reached the top, pushing open a green door to the bright rooftop of the Ravjek courthouse.

The green dome towered above them on the far side of a helipad. The massive King Stallion was moving into position to land. Four men waited on the roof. Fitzsimmons stood alongside a pair of Vakovian soldiers and a man Shane recognized from his appearances on the television.

"This is the President," Radek said. "He is the one responsible for bringing in these Reapers? For Oleg?"

"Yeah," Shane said. "Looks like."

Radek scowled. President Janosik held a briefcase in one hand while the other held a floppy, olive beret atop his head. He wore something akin to a military uniform adorned with medals Shane was certain he hadn't earned, waiting for the chopper to land.

"Soldiers first," Shane said to Radek, barely audible above the chopper. The ghost nodded and ran at the armed men while Shane made a beeline for Fitzsimmons.

Even with one hand, Radek was brutally efficient. He broke the first soldier's neck in seconds and was on to the second one before Janosik or Fitzsimmons noticed.

The major turned in time to see Shane storming toward him. He said something, the words lost in the helicopter's rumble, and Shane threw a punch.

Fitzsimmons took the hit well, stumbling just a bit before returning the favor. He took a shot at Shane's midsection and then went for the face. He and Cuddy must have sparred together, their fighting style was nearly identical. Fitzsimmons wasn't in great shape, but he had learned technique, and he knew how to defend as well as attack.

The two men traded blows as Shane held in winces and groans. His body was depleted, bruised, and beaten from too many previous encounters. Fitzsimmons was fresh and ready and not holding back.

The helicopter descended slowly, the pilot unsure of what to do as he saw Shane and the major going at it. A half-heard scream drew Shane's attention, and Janosik's beret skidded to his feet as the man fell, clutching a bloody mouth. Radek was taking his time.

As far as Shane knew, Janosik could not see spirits. Radek's backhand had come from nowhere, and the President fell hard, spitting blood. His face looked panicked as he crawled away. Radek's boot took him in the backside, knocking him flat to his gut.

Fitzsimmons pummeled Shane's side below the ribs, pounding already bruised and damaged tissue. Shane twisted to defend himself, but the major was moving faster. Knuckles cracked against Shane's jaw, and his head jerked as blood and spit sprayed across the rooftop.

"You thought you could fight me like this?" the major yelled over the roar of the King Stallion. "You can barely stand."

A boot hit Shane in the knee, and he gritted his teeth, holding back a howl of pain. Nothing had broken, but it forced him to the ground. He crumpled onto Janosik's beret, spitting into it as Radek shouted something he couldn't hear.

Fitzsimmons raised his boot, and Shane growled, looking up at him.

"Goodbye, Ryan," the man said. Shane said nothing. Radek's form crashed into Fitzsimmons and tackled him just as the helicopter landed. Shane had the President's beret in his hands, and he spit again, clearing his head before a boot stepped on his fingers.

"That is mine, sir," a thickly accented voice said in English.

Janosik was on his feet again. He held a pistol aimed at Shane's head. Shane smiled up at him through bloody teeth and raised his free hand in compliance. Janosik removed his boot and gestured with the gun. Slowly, Shane picked up the beret and handed it to him.

A ghost appeared from the helicopter, the pilot's spectral asset, and rushed Radek as Janosik ran to the open doors and boarded.

The two ghosts fought, giving Fitzsimmons time to get to his feet. He made just two steps toward the helicopter before Janosik closed the doors and the aircraft lifted off again. Fitzsimmons cursed loudly and Shane laughed, standing up.

"Missed your ride?" Shane called out. The major looked back at him and pulled a gun from his hip.

"I won't miss you," he shouted back.

Shane made a run for the stairwell door. The gun went off, and he felt a searing pain through his left shoulder. The force of the hit caused him to fall forward, saving his life as a second shot hit the wall where he had been a heartbeat earlier.

He crawled forward as quickly as he could, blood leaking from the bullet hole in his shoulder, and looked back. Fitzsimmons was coming for him, gun raised. Shane pulled at the edge of the top step and rolled down, narrowly avoiding a third gunshot.

His body banged down each step to the next landing, and he groaned, scrambling for the next set of stairs as Fitzsimmons fired two more shots from the top of the steps. One grazed his leg, and the other hit the step as Shane rolled once more.

"I'm sending you back home in a box, Ryan," Fitzsimmons yelled down the stairs as he reloaded.

Shane pulled himself to his feet and leaned on the railing to head down the next flight.

Fitzsimmons was injured enough that he could not chase Shane down the steps at full speed, but he was still coming. Outside, the sound of gunfire continued to shake the courthouse walls. Shane had only one idea for a potential escape that might keep him alive.

He stumbled down steps, falling several more times. Two more shots rang out, but Fitzsimmons missed with each one, if only by inches. If he got a clear shot at some point, it was over for Shane.

Radek was still missing in action, either tangling with the helicopter pilot's ghost or something else. Shane could not rely on him for the assist. He made his way to the basement, back the way he had come.

With bloody and weak hands, Shane pulled open the basement door and stumbled down the hallway. The wound in his shoulder bled freely, leaving a trail across the floor that dripped from his fingers. He wasn't worried about it. The hallway from the stairs was a good length, long enough that he would still be in it when Fitzsimmons entered as well. The man would have a clear shot.

Shane hobbled, his knee swollen, his shoulder throbbing, and his entire body aching. He approached the hole in the wall that led to the dungeon and leaned against the exposed edge to catch his breath.

"Ryan," Fitzsimmons shouted. He was in the hallway, steps from the stairway entrance. His gun was raised, aimed, and ready. Shane turned and smiled. Fitzsimmons pulled the trigger.

Shane fell through the busted doorway.

CHAPTER 27
AFTERLIFE

Fitzsimmons gritted his teeth, holding back a victorious growl. He lowered his sidearm and watched Shane Ryan's body fall backward into an open doorway. He wasn't sure he'd hit him at first, but finally, blessedly, the man was down. He was so sick of him and the trouble he'd caused.

The major approached the doorway with caution, eager to put a final bullet in Shane Ryan's head but not so eager that he was going to be reckless. He kept the gun drawn at his side and ready.

The attack outside the courthouse continued, even as that coward Janosik fled in Fitzsimmons' helicopter. If he ever saw the man again, he'd shoot him himself.

He reached the doorway, only it wasn't a doorway at all. Someone had broken a hole through the hallway, from the inside, revealing a hidden passage. A stairway led down into the dark, some kind of secret sub-basement below the courthouse.

Fitzsimmons kept his gun ready and peered into the hole in the wall. Stone steps were all he could see in the light from the hall. Ryan's body was missing, though. There was blood on the landing and the first step. He'd escaped into the dark.

Fitzsimmons sighed. He was really starting to hate Ryan. His gut told him to let it go, that the man would bleed out in the dark, and that would be the end of it. But he couldn't make himself believe it. Ryan had survived weeks in the Vakovian wilderness. He'd fought off dozens of Reapers. The son of a bitch was almost immortal, it seemed. But bullets worked. Bullets hurt him. So, Fitzsimmons needed to end it.

He stepped through the hole and into the dark. There was no sound from below, and the light was so faint that he couldn't even see how many stairs were laid out or if Ryan was dead at the bottom of them.

Fitzsimmons reached into his pocket and pulled out his phone. He swiped the screen and then pressed the button to activate the flashlight.

A crowd of the dead stood at the bottom of the stone steps and Fitzsimmons' breath caught. He hadn't expected to see so many, especially not so many in the condition they were in. The ghosts were like nightmares, beaten and bloody. Some were like monsters, with flesh and bone exposed and only madness in their eyes.

"Jesus," he whispered.

"Try again," someone answered.

Ryan stepped out from behind the dungeon door and pushed Fitzsimmons. The major fell forward, tumbling down the stairs as his phone and gun clattered down the stone steps with him.

The ghosts of the dungeon were on him in seconds. Cold hands and teeth ripped at his flesh. Bones broke and tissue tore. Fitzsimmons screamed and watched as Shane Ryan pulled the door closed behind him as he returned to the courthouse basement.

✳ ✳ ✳

Shane slumped against the wall. Fitzsimmons' screams cut off abruptly, and the hallway was silent again. Only the sounds of a fight outside, muffled gunfire that sounded so far away, came to his ears now.

"Shane!"

Radek came for him, running awkwardly. The ghost was missing an eye now, and his left leg was badly broken. The pilot's ghost had maimed him, and Shane knew such wounds were permanent for a spirit.

"Fitzsimmons?"

"Down there," Shane said with a smile. Radek nodded.

"I had trouble finding you," the ghost said. "You don't have my pin anymore."

"I don't," Shane replied. "I saw you were busy up on the roof, and that Janosik was going to get away."

"That ugly hat," the ghost said. Shane laughed.

"That ugly hat."

Before Janosik had taken the beret back from Shane, Shane had pinned the small, silver coat of arms that held Radek's spirit to it. The ghost seemed keen on revenge, and Shane wanted to make sure he had it.

"He's not gone yet, but soon enough, the helicopter will be out of range. You can find him there," Shane said. Once the President had fled at least a mile, Radek would be forced to follow. It was an impromptu goodbye, but neither of them was in good shape, and Shane needed to leave Vakovia as soon as he could.

"Don't let him get that far," Radek said. He rested his good hand on Shane's uninjured shoulder. He only had one eye left, but it stared straight into Shane's.

"Are you sure?" Shane asked.

"Look at me," the ghost replied. He was falling apart. His fighting days were over. Shane had thought he could still try his hand at revenge in person. "Be quick."

Shane sighed.

"It was an honor to fight at your side, soldier," he said.

"The honor was mine," Radek replied.

Shane raised his hands and held the ghost's head between them.

"He's going to be so surprised," Radek laughed. Shane laughed and pressed his hands together.

Radek's head crumbled and burst. Shane groaned in pain as he fell backward and hit the floor hard. Somewhere, in the skies over Ravjek, the

President's head exploded, too.

* * *

"Look at this mess, American."

Shane opened his eyes, and Vanko was kneeling over him. Another man helped the Russian get him to his feet. His shirt had been cut off and his shoulder was bandaged. He was on the first floor of the courthouse near the entrance now. Other men were milling about, some soldiers and some not.

"Is that Zemba?" Shane asked. Peter Zemba was within a small crowd. People ran back and forth around him, and many other bodies were being attended to by medics. The courthouse lobby had morphed into a rudimentary combat hospital.

"That is Zemba," Vanko said. "President Janosik is dead. Some sniper took him out in a helicopter. Blew his head clean off, can you believe that?"

"I can," Shane said. "The guy was an asshole."

Vanko laughed and slapped Shane on the back, sending a shockwave of pain through his body.

Zemba, drawn to the sound of the Russian's laughter, approached them with aides at his side. He held out his hand and smiled at Ryan.

"Mr. Ryan. I am happy to see you again. Still alive!" he said.

"As are you," Shane replied. "You taking over now, or…?"

"There will be an election," Zemba said. "A fair one, this time. Then we shall see."

"Sir," one of the aides said, handing Zemba a manila envelope. The man's eyes lit up, and he took it then gave it to Shane.

"A gift," he said.

Shane opened the envelope and pulled out his passport and a pack of cigarettes, along with several stacks of money that were taken from his hotel room. He took the cigarettes and passport as well as a few dollars, and handed the rest to Vanko.

"For your troubles," he said, popping a cigarette into his mouth.

"You are such a good customer," Vanko said, pocketing the money.

"I have arranged for you to get a flight home," Zemba said. "Your involvement in any terrorist plots has also been cleared up with your country's embassy. Other than perhaps some unfortunate internet search results that may plague you, your name is clear."

Shane lit the cigarette and took a sustained drag, then exhaled slowly. It had been too long.

"You work fast," Shane said. He couldn't have been unconscious all that long. Now he was on his way home with a clear name. Nothing in Vakovia had seemed that efficient before. Maybe Zemba really would turn the place around.

"It was a top priority. No offense, Mr. Ryan, but everyone wants you gone. The doctor tells me you can travel in just a few days," the man said.

"Fair enough," he replied. He had overstayed his welcome, anyway. A few days was an acceptable timeline. The Reapers were done in Vakovia, but they were not gone yet. Whoever pulled the strings was back home.

Shane had not gotten the answers he wanted from Fitzsimmons. He would have to get them from someone else.

Epilogue

Carl watched the world from the third-story window. Cars drove down Berkley Street, and people walked their dogs. The noise of the town came faintly to the house, a sort of dull thrum of life.

Shane had been gone for nearly two months. He had never been away from home for so long without having explained what was happening. His trip abroad was going to be a week or two at most.

The sun was setting, and though there was no reason to expect that, if Shane came home, it would be during daylight hours, the end of another day brought more dread to Carl's mind. He was not prepared to admit such a thing openly, but he was not blind to the possibility that Shane was not coming back.

As strong and resourceful as Shane was, he was not indestructible. No one was. An accident could end him as easily as any other mortal man. But given the nature of his trip, it was more likely he'd cross someone and couldn't overcome the odds. Whoever killed his friend Blakely could have killed him as well.

People had come looking for Shane. James Moran had come to the house twice. Frank had come by as well.

"Are you well, Carl?" Herbert asked.

"No," he answered.

Herbert was still new to the house. He did not know Shane well. He did not know any of them well. He seemed a nice enough man, and Shane had explained how the large spirit had been integral to keeping him alive when they met. But he was still an outsider to Carl.

"I would like to say I'm sure he's alright, and that he will be back soon.

But I imagine that you and I know better than most that no one can truthfully say things like that."

"Indeed, Herbert," Carl said. The days kept ticking by.

If Shane did not come home, Carl was not sure what would happen. To the house, to the others. To himself. All of that seemed so very insignificant, though.

"It's funny. I've only known him a short time compared to you, but I've had this sense since we met that Shane's not supposed to die. I know he's just a man but... does that make sense?"

Carl looked at Herbert and smiled.

"It does," he replied. He had struggled with the same nonsense idea. Shane was just a man. But in some ways, he was not. He was something unlike anyone Carl had heard of. He straddled the line between life and death every day. He was not supposed to die.

The sun set, and the two ghosts watched Nashua embrace the darkness. They could stand there for days if need be. It made no difference to either of them.

The last hints of light were long gone. It was past midnight when Eloise came to the room, rushing from the depths of the house.

"Someone is here," she said to Carl.

"A visitor?" Carl wondered. He had seen no one approach along the front walkway. And it was very late in any event.

"No," Eloise said sternly. "They are not visitors."

Carl looked at Herbert and the three ghosts left together, descending through the house to the main floor.

From the shadows of the dark house, Carl could see that Eloise was not mistaken. Four intruders had already broken in through the garden door. But they were not all men. Not living ones, anyway. Two living and two spirits, working together.

The living men were dressed identically in black. They were not in military uniforms, but Carl recognized their movements and the gear they carried well enough to know they were trained soldiers. They moved stealthily and used night-vision goggles to find their way through the house.

The ghosts were clearly partnered with the men, one to one. Shane had left to investigate his friend Blakely's group in Vakovia. It was no coincidence. But if they were breaking into Shane's house in the middle of the night, then it meant something significant. It meant Shane was not dead.

A radio crackled faintly and one of the men stopped, gently pressing an earpiece.

"This is Diggs," the man said.

The radio voice was tinny and hard to make out, but Carl heard it mention "a spirit in the window". Someone had been watching him from outside.

"Proceeding," the man called Diggs answered. He nodded to the other living man and they split up, each taking their ghost partner. Diggs made his way to the stairs while the other man made his way to the kitchen.

The wood of the house groaned. It was unhappy to have unwelcome guests. Carl could feel the building moving, a sort of unconscious sense he had developed over the years. The floor plan of the house was changing.

Diggs got too far ahead of the ghost companion with him. Carl, within the walls alongside Eloise and Herbert, watched the man turn a corner. The hallway sealed behind him. He was on the second floor now, and his ghost companion was still on the first. It took him only a few seconds to notice, but by then, it was too late.

"The other one," Carl whispered to Eloise, indicating the soldier heading to the kitchen. The girl nodded and drifted away through shadows as Carl followed the man who was now on the second floor. Herbert stayed behind, watching the ghost to see where it went.

"Alvarez, this is Diggs. I've got some weird movement here," the man said, trying to find the hallway where he and his ghost had just been. No one replied over the radio.

"Alvarez," he said again. Still nothing.

The hallway meandered through the house, taking the intruder farther and farther from the stairs that would lead him back to his companions. Carl drifted through the spaces between the walls, emerging here and there to watch the man as he puzzled over directions that no longer made sense to him.

Finally, the man found himself in a hallway that even Carl didn't recognize. It was short and devoid of doors save for one at the very end. Carl recognized that door.

The man opened the door slowly. The hinges remained silent and although it was dark, Carl knew what he would see through his night vision. The library.

"Alvarez. Rictor!" the man said. No one was even on the same floor.

He stepped into the library, but Carl had already circled around. The lights in the room came on and the man flinched, covering his eyes as he pulled the goggles away before they blinded him.

Carl stood next to a bookcase watching him. The intruder lifted his head, eyes squinting from the sudden burst of light, and then saw he was not alone.

"Hold it right there," the soldier ordered, training a gun on Carl. Carl smiled, amused by the man's threat.

"The library isn't usually on this side of the house, did you know that?" Carl asked. He had been in the same situation once before in the same room, only he was standing in the soldier's place at that time, and Mr. Anderson was where Carl stood.

"You're coming with us," the soldier said.

Carl ignored him and moved his hand to a hidden switch. The bookcase rolled back away from the wall, and the intruder raised his rifle to his eye.

"Come have a look," he said.

"Tell me where your anchor item is. Now," the man said.

Carl raised an eyebrow.

"Or what? Will you shoot me?"

The soldier's jaw tensed.

"Rictor! I got eyes on target. I need you here now!" the man yelled.

"We probably have a moment before your ghostly friend arrives. You should really have a look. Have you ever seen an oubliette?"

The soldier didn't move. Carl turned away from him and looked down the hole hidden away in the wall. It was where Anderson had pushed him all those years ago. It was where he died.

"What you're looking for is down there," Carl pointed out.

The soldier moved slowly and cautiously, still foolishly keeping his gun trained on Carl.

"Back away," the man said.

Carl did as instructed. The soldier moved toward the hole and glanced down. In the dark, it was impossible to see anything.

"There's nothing—" the man began. He turned his head, and Carl was almost nose-to-nose with him.

"Nothing there? I assure you there is," Carl stated.

"You think you're going to drop me down there? Think again, spook," the man said snidely.

He stabbed Carl in the gut with a length of iron rod. Carl felt his body stretch from within, and instantly, he was at the bottom of the hole, next to his bones once more. It took him seconds to get back to the man, behind him this time.

"I had no intention of dropping you in there," Carl said, catching the man's wrist before he could stab him again. "That's *my* place."

The soldier struggled as Carl pulled him close, wrapping an arm around his head from behind and then twisting sharply. The man's neck snapped, and his body slumped to the floor. Carl left to see what had become of the second intruder.

* * *

Alvarez slowly scanned the kitchen. He had heard a door opening, but there was no one around. A hinge creaked again, from somewhere out in the hall this time, and he doubled back in search of it.

He had lost Diggs and Rictor, and he could no longer see Lamber, his spectral asset, either. So far, nothing in the house indicated anyone was there, living or dead, either.

Something thumped, and he followed the sound to a pantry. A trapdoor in the floor was open, leading into the darkness of a cellar below. He stood over it, staring down, and adjusted the goggles on his eyes. Something was malfunctioning. The night vision was not piercing the shadows of the cellar. He could see nothing.

"Garbage equipment," he muttered, stripping them off, and pulling a small flashlight from his belt. He clicked it on and headed down the wooden steps into the space below the house.

"Diggs, I'm heading to the cellar," he said over the radio. The other man did not respond.

"Diggs," he said again. Still no reply.

Something shuffled in the cellar. Alvarez let the radio go and lifted his weapon, holding the flashlight in the other hand and scanning the dark. There were shelves full of ancient jars, caked in dust and cobwebs, but he could see little else.

Slowly, Alvarez made his way deeper into the darkness. The beam of the light swept back and forth. It seemed like some of the shadows were slow to move away from the light at first, but in a blink, the effect was gone.

A slithering sound filled the void, and Alvarez turned sharply, sweeping left to right along the wall. He saw nothing but his shadow and then paused, staring at it. He was holding the light in his hand. He couldn't have been casting a shadow in front of himself.

His shadow raised a hand and waved. Then the flashlight bulb popped, and darkness overwhelmed him.

Alvarez ran for the stairs as something pulled at his leg. He got to his knees, and it pulled again, forcing him flat to his stomach.

"Nowhere to go," a quiet voice hissed in his ear.

A hand like ice clasped his ankle and sharp, needling claws dug into his flesh. He screamed as it pulled him deeper into the dark.

✻ ✻ ✻

Carl arrived at the butler's pantry just as one of the Davis sisters closed the trapdoor to the cellar.

"I heard a scream," he said, entering the room.

"He'll be done soon," Eloise said. She and the sisters were watching. The sound faded away from under the trapdoor until the house was silent.

"There are two spirits with them," Carl pointed out.

"Not anymore," Herbert said, joining the others with Thaddeus.

"They tried to hurt me, but Herbert ripped them apart," the boy said, entertained by the whole ordeal. Carl, however, was not.

"These men and their ghosts were looking to take me, probably even all of us, from the house," he pointed out. Carl had been kidnapped once already, by a very powerful being. He did not intend to go through such a thing ever again.

"Who were they?" Eloise asked.

"The men who Shane went to find, I think," Carl said.

Eloise looked worried and glanced at the sisters and Herbert before focusing on Carl again.

"Why would they come here, then? Does that mean something has happened to Shane Ryan?"

The men had been speaking to someone outside on the radio, at least one person but probably more. There was a chance they would leave when they could no longer contact their men inside. There was also a chance that more would come looking.

"If these men are here now, I think Shane found them. And I think he's on his way home," Carl said.

He did not expect it was going to be a happy homecoming.

Check out these best-selling series from our talented authors:

GHOST STORIES

RON RIPLEY
BERKLEY STREET SERIES
MOVING IN SERIES
HAUNTED COLLECTION SERIES
DEATH HUNTER SERIES

IAN FORTEY
JIGSAW OF SOULS SERIES
CULT OF THE ENDLESS NIGHT SERIES

SUPERNATURAL SUSPENSE

A. I. NASSER
SLAUGHTER SERIES
SIN SERIES

DAVID LONGHORN
NIGHTMARE SERIES
ASYLUM SERIES

SARA CLANCY
THE BELL WITCH SERIES
BANSHEE SERIES

For a complete list of our new releases and best-selling horror books, visit ScareStreet.com or scan the QR code below!

Printed in Great Britain
by Amazon